BARBARY WHARF

Harlequin Presents and bestselling author Charlotte Lamb welcome you to the world of Barbary Wharf.

In this fascinating saga, you'll experience all the intrigue and glamour of the international world of journalism. You'll watch the inner workings of a newsroom, share the secrets discussed behind closed doors, travel to the most thrilling cities in the world. Join the players in this high-stakes game as they gamble for the biggest prize of all—true love.

You've met Nick Caspian and Gina Tyrrell, whose dramatic story of passion and heartache unfolds throughout this series. And you've followed the relationships of four couples—Hazel Forbes and Piet van Leyden, Roz Amery and Daniel Bruneille, Irena Olivero and Esteban Sebastian, and Valerie Knight and Gib Collingwood—as each fell in love. Now join Sophie Watson and Guy Faulkner to discover if love on the rebound can be the real thing.

Don't miss these unforgettable romantic adventures each month in Harlequin Presents—the bestselling romance fiction series in the world.

The Editors

THE SENTINEL

PRINTING PLANT EMPLOYEES THREATEN STRIKE ACTION

LONDON—Electricians and machinists at the *Sentinel*'s Barbary Wharf printing plant met today with management representatives from the paper in the wake of proposed staff cuts. Inside sources say workers plan strike action—a move that could cost the *Sentinel* millions of dollars in lost revenue—if the cuts are approved by *Sentinel* head Nick Caspian. Prior to the paper's move to Barbary Wharf last year, Caspian modernized the printing process, which cut hundreds of traditional printing craft jobs. He blames this further loss of jobs on the general recession in Britain and Europe. Printing staff claim they are already operating with the absolute minimum number of workers. Talks are expected to continue well into the night.

GINA TYRRELL BACK WITH MAC?

LONDON—Conflict of interest? Apparently not for newspaperwoman Gina Tyrrell. Judging from recent sightings of Ms. Tyrrell and actor Mac Cameron, she doesn't seem the slightest bit concerned that the outcome of the *Sentinel*'s legal battle with Mr. Cameron is still pending. Ms. Tyrrell and Mr. Cameron, who have had an on-again off-again relationship, were recently spotted attending the opening of Barry Eagle's new downtown nightclub, The Blue Penguin. Perhaps Mr. Cameron's lawsuit against the *Sentinel* will be settled out of court....

A Sweet Addiction

BARBARY WHARF

Harlequin Books

TORONTO • NEW YORK • LONDON
AMSTERDAM • PARIS • SYDNEY • HAMBURG
STOCKHOLM • ATHENS • TOKYO • MILAN
MADRID • WARSAW • BUDAPEST • AUCKLAND

Harlequin Presents first edition February 1993
ISBN 0-373-11530-X

Original hardcover edition published in 1992
by Mills & Boon Limited

A SWEET ADDICTION

BARBARY WHARF

For more than one hundred years, London's Fleet Street has been the heartbeat of Britain's major newspaper and magazine industries. But decaying buildings and the high cost of inner-city real estate have forced many companies to relocate dockside, down by the Thames River.

The owner of one such company, Sir George Tyrrell, had a dream, a vision of leading his newspaper, the *Sentinel*, into the twenty-first century with a huge, ultramodern complex called Barbary Wharf. But without additional money and time, the dream—and perhaps even the newspaper—will die.

Enter Nick Caspian, international media tycoon. The man with all the desire and the money to take over the *Sentinel*. Now, as joint owners of the paper, Nick Caspian and Gina Tyrrell are often at odds . . . but they are *always* acutely aware of each other as man and woman. Lately they've become inseparable. But the appearance of a key player on the *Sentinel*'s board of directors indicates that the power struggle has really just begun.

Meanwhile, secretary Sophie Watson struggles to avoid the affair that Guy Faulkner, her handsome boss, considers *unavoidable*. And his lawyer's instincts have never let him down before. . . .

BARBARY WHARF

CAST OF CHARACTERS

Guy Faulkner—The *Sentinel*'s sophisticated lawyer. He has recently realized that his career has become his whole life. It's time to devote some attention to outside pursuits—it's time to fall in love.

Sophie Watson—Guy Faulkner's young and impressionable assistant. Her hopes of love seem destined to be destroyed now that Gib Collingwood, a man she has long been attracted to, has become engaged to award-winning feature writer, Valerie Knight.

Gina Tyrrell—The young widow of Sir George Tyrrell's beloved grandson. Devastated by her husband's death, she devoted herself entirely to Sir George's well-being. And now she will devote herself entirely to his paper, the *Sentinel*.

Nick Caspian—International media tycoon with playboy reputation. Owns and operates newspapers all over Europe, and has now set his sights on Britain. Whatever Nick Caspian wants, he usually gets...and right now he wants the *Sentinel and* Gina Tyrrell... possibly in that order.

Mac Cameron—International star of stage and screen. He has the reputation of being a merciless lady-killer. Mac is suing the *Sentinel* for what he contends is a false report claiming that he fathered a young woman's child.

Andreas Kirk—A powerful and extrememly enigmatic lawyer. He is a man who is not too proud to mix with members of the criminal underworld. He is obviously pursuing Sophie Watson, although his motives for his sudden interest are not as easily discerned.

CHAPTER ONE

IT HAD never been so hard to smile. Sophie didn't know how she managed it; her face kept stiffening and her jaw ached. She hardly noticed who she was talking to, except that they were all from the *Sentinel*, and mostly editorial people. She nodded and smiled, sometimes even spoke, although heaven alone knew what she said. She certainly didn't. She was just waiting for her chance to make an excuse and leave the party without anyone suspecting why.

'Having fun, Sophie?' someone asked, coming up behind her.

She started and turned, her amber eyes wide, then recognised Tom Birny, a husky, broad-shouldered crime reporter she often saw at work, and forced another of her meaningless smiles. 'Hi, Tom! Yes, I'm having a great time,' she lied. 'Are you?'

'I'd enjoy it more if you'd dance with me,' he said, grinning at her, then someone yelled for him from the other side of the room and he groaned. 'I've been spotted! I'll have to go, I've been roped in to help with a little joke they're going to play on Gib. Save me a dance later?'

He vanished before she had to reply, and she sighed. Tom had asked her out several times, but she had never accepted because she was a one-man woman and she had only been interested in Gilbey Collingwood.

The first she'd known of Gilbey's engagement to Valerie Knight had been when the invitation to their engagement party had arrived. That had been their way of telling everyone.

She had crumpled it up, sobbing angrily. But her pride couldn't stand the idea of anyone guessing how she felt,

7

especially Gib, so she had had to come and try to look as if she hadn't a care in the world.

She glanced across the room, to where they were dancing, cheek to cheek, Valerie Knight's blonde head nestling on Gib's shoulder. She might have been able to bear it if the two of them didn't look so impossibly happy. Did she have to cling to him like that? And did Gib have to hold her quite so close? Did they have to make it so obvious that they were crazy about each other?

Pain stabbed inside her as she suddenly met Gib's eyes over Valerie's head, and he smiled, that familiar, warm, intimate smile she had once hoped might mean he was coming to care about her. It hadn't, of course. All it had meant was that Gib liked her and was a friendly man.

After a second of sheer anguish, she managed to smile back, hoping he couldn't see strain in her face, then she hurriedly turned away, as if looking for someone, only to bump into her boss.

'Drunk already?' he teased and then looked into her face and stopped smiling, dark brows lowering into a frown. 'Sophie! For God's sake!'

She struggled to hold back tears, knowing she was white, her body trembling. 'I've got a headache,' she lied shakily.

She had the feeling Guy Faulkner did not believe her. A tall, thin man with dark hair and a clever face, he was a lawyer, trained to pick up lies and evasions, his hard blue eyes penetrating.

'I think we'd better get you out of here,' he said in curt tones, and startled her by putting both arms around her and dragging her close to him.

'What...?' she spluttered, and then his hand clamped down on her golden-brown hair, pushing her face down into his shoulder.

Before she could struggle he was dancing her through the crowd of people in the big room towards the exit, their bodies apparently welded together. Sophie had never realised how powerful his thin body was; she could feel every inch of it moving against her, gliding and twisting sensually, while controlling her as if she were a rag doll all at the same time.

What must it look like? she thought wildly, helpless in his grip. People would raise their eyebrows, seeing her and Guy dancing like lovers. It would cause gossip, and Sophie loathed the idea of being talked about.

Well, let them talk! said another part of her mind. Anything was better than being pitied; she would hate it if they ever suspected she loved Gib. It had been bad enough listening to some of the girls dreamily reminiscing about dates with Gib before he'd turned serious about Valerie. At least they hadn't asked her any probing questions. They had probably assumed she and Gib were just good friends. Sophie had never been the kind to pour out her feelings to anyone, and she had no close friends on the newspaper she might have confided in.

Guy whirled her out of the room; leaving behind the noise and disco lights, the throb of the music, the loud voices. He stopped dancing and let go of her, looking down, his eyes narrowed and searching. She was flushed and breathless now, and faintly dizzy.

'Get your coat from the cloakroom, and I'll see you back here in five minutes, and drive you home,' he ordered, turned on his heel and vanished into the men's cloakroom.

Sophie's teeth met. She didn't want Guy Faulkner taking her home. He would probably ask questions; he was good at that, it was part of his job on the *Sentinel*, checking out all the angles of a story to make sure the newspaper could not be sued over it. Guy on the scent of the truth could be formidable, and she had seen him in action too often to want to have his techniques applied to her.

She had to get her coat, though; she was going to need it on the way home. It was only the start of December, but it was bitterly cold, and snow had been in the air all afternoon. Sitting at her desk, she had watched the white flakes floating and drifting down, and shivered, thinking that this was going to be a hard winter in more ways than one.

She found several other girls in the ladies' powder-room, brushing their hair, renewing lipstick, checking on their stockings.

'Enjoying the party, Sophie?' asked a girl with blue eyes and razor-cut black hair, turning to smile at her, a lipstick in her hand.

'Oh, hello, Roz,' Sophie managed huskily, forcing a smile back. 'Yes, it's a good party, isn't it? What a fabulous dress! You look terrific in it, too!'

'Thanks, I always love wearing it,' Roz Amery said, glancing at her own reflection in the mirror with bright-eyed pleasure. She was slight, with a boyish figure, and the 1920-style dress was perfect for her: poppy-red, shimmering with sequins, it barely reached her knees although it had a silky fringe at the hem, making her slender legs look longer and more elegant. 'You look gorgeous, yourself,' she said, watching Sophie in the mirror. 'Very elegant—a Hamnett dress, isn't it?'

Sophie was brushing her lids with amber shadow, erasing a faint pinkness which was the only trace of her tears.

'Yes, that's right,' she said, concentrating on her task. She had bought the yellow wool-silk Katharine Hamnett dress that morning in London's Bond Street, determined to look her best at the engagement party, as if she hadn't a care in the world. Not for her the drama and panache of Roz's outfit; she couldn't carry off anything like that. She chose classy, elegant clothes with good lines and clear, cool colours. They were expensive, but they lasted forever, if you looked after them.

'I wonder if Valerie and Gib are going to settle down now?' Roz murmered drily. 'They both have pretty lively pasts, don't they? I was looking round the room, and lost count of their old flames. Do you think it will last between them?'

'I couldn't begin to guess!' Sophie muttered, tidying her smooth chignon of gold-brown hair. She didn't comfort herself with the hope that this engagement might break up. There was something too possessive and satisfied in the way Gib had been holding Valerie Knight; he had worn the look of a man who had finally got what he wanted and wasn't giving it up.

'Well, they make a handsome couple,' Roz said, closing her silver evening bag with a little snap.

'Yes,' said Sophie, watching herself in the mirror for betraying signs, but nobody could read anything from her face now. The mask was firmly in place.

The other girls went out, leaving just Sophic and Roz, and, trying to change the subject, Sophie remembered some gossip she had heard earlier.

'Is it true that you've been offered the Paris job?' she asked, and Roz did a double-take.

'Who told you that?' she asked sharply.

'Oh, it was being talked about in the party.' Actually, Sophie had heard it from one of the junior secretaries in the proprietor's office, a girl who had overheard a conversation.

'How do these things get out?' Roz muttered angrily. 'Nick Caspian only sent for me this morning!'

'Walls have ears at Barbary Wharf!' Sophie said lightly.

'Tongues as well, unfortunately!' Roz bit out. 'Well, just between you and me, and please don't repeat this, I haven't actually accepted yet, and I'm not sure I want the job, but it's true, he did offer it to me.'

She was one of the *Sentinel*'s roving foreign correspondents, jokingly known as 'visiting firemen' and sent wherever a story broke out in a part of the world where the newspaper didn't have a permanent correspondent.

Looking at her sympathetically, Sophie said, 'You've always wanted a permanent job abroad, haven't you?

But now, if you accept this one, it would make things difficult for you and Daniel, wouldn't it? It isn't easy to commute between London and Paris all the time.'

Roz sighed. 'No. Ask Hazel van Leyden how easy it is to be married to a man who lives in another country!'

'Especially when you're pregnant!' agreed Sophie. 'What is she going to do when she has the baby? Will her husband come back here to live, or will she move over to Holland?'

'I've no idea. I don't think she has decided what to do, yet.' Roz sighed. 'Why is life so complicated?' She turned towards the door. 'I'd better get back to Daniel.'

Once she had gone, Sophie was alone, briefly, staring into the mirror and seeing past her mask. This had been the longest day of her life, but it was almost over, thank heavens. She felt drained and empty, too tired even to weep.

Then the door opened and Colette Tse, the impassively beautiful features editor, walked in, giving her a nod before disappearing into one of the cubicles. Sophie didn't want to talk to anyone else. She left, collecting her coat on the way out.

Guy Faulkner was waiting outside. His blue gaze flicked over her, from head to foot, and she stiffened resentfully.

'There's no need for you to see me home. I can take a taxi!'

'I am taking you,' Guy informed her with dry emphasis.

'I can take myself! I brought myself here, after all!'

His mouth tightened, but he didn't go on arguing. He just fastened an iron grip around her arm and propelled her along the corridor, towards the lift.

She considered struggling, protesting, but she needed all her will-power to hold back her tears, so she gave in reluctantly, glaring at him. The lift doors closed and they dropped down to the underground car park.

The party was being held in a hospitality suite on the first floor of the newly built Barbary Wharf Hotel, part of the riverside complex which housed the offices and printing works of the *Sentinel* newspaper. The hotel had only been finished and opened that autumn, and was the latest phase of the building operation begun by the previous owner of the *Sentinel*, Sir George Tyrrell, who had died about a year ago, during a power struggle between himself and Nick Caspian, the European Press tycoon who now controlled the *Sentinel*.

What had once been a grim, depressed area on the banks of the Thames, a crumbling wharf, empty, run-down warehouses, a few grey, grimy, boarded-up houses, had been turned into a busy, thriving little city within a city.

Barbary Wharf was self-contained: it had its own post office, bank, travel agent, shops, hairdressers, restaurants, bars, and now it even had its own small hotel. It had been necessary for the development of the site to include all those facilities because when they had moved from Fleet Street eastwards along the river they had entered a district where there was virtually no social infrastructure. Everything had had to be put in place from scratch.

The lift shot down rapidly, the doors opened and Guy urged her out. His ice-blue Volvo was parked near by. He unlocked it, helped her into the front passenger-seat and a moment later drove up out of the car park into North Street, the side of Barbary Wharf which was furthest from the river.

It was a clear, cloudless night, but bitterly cold, with ice on the roads, and few people around in the streets. Guy had driven her home once before, after they had worked very late, since he lived quite close to her. So he did not need to ask for directions, turning west, with the river on their right and London Bridge ahead of them.

Sophie lived in the basement of a Victorian house in Chelsea which belonged to an uncle, a Hungarian writer who worked at the BBC part-time, and had for years been writing a modern history of his country. Uncle Theo had bought the house very cheaply, just after the Second World War, from the sale of his dead mother's jewellery, which he had smuggled out in his shoes when he fled. His aristocratic Hungarian family had once been fabulously wealthy. Now the Chelsea house provided him with his main income.

He didn't earn much from the BBC, and very little from writing, so the money from the house was essential to him. He let out each floor as a separate flat at very high rents; but since Sophie was his sister's daughter he only charged her a nominal rent, well within her capacity to pay, and in return Sophie worked for him in her spare time, putting his Hungarian research on to computer discs so that he could store it and retrieve it without difficulty, typing up his manuscript, answering his letters. Uncle Theo couldn't afford to pay a secretary.

When Guy turned into the road he slowed. 'Which number was it?' She told him, and he pulled up outside, and looked at the tall, gabled house. 'Which floor are you on?' he asked curiously, glancing upwards.

'The basement.'

His gaze dropped down again, his face quizzical. 'Isn't that dreary? There can't be much light down there, and no view at all.'

'I like it,' she crossly defended. 'OK, the windows are tiny, but I've given it a Mediterranean look with a lot of white paint, curtains and cushions in primary colours, and a few prints of Impressionist paintings. It looks great.'

'I'd love to see it,' he drawled, and she stiffened.

'Not tonight; sorry!' she snapped, and his brows shot up.

'I wasn't fishing for an invitation! You're in a difficult mood tonight, aren't you?'

She looked down, flushing. She had always prided herself on being the perfect secretary, calm, polite, unflappable, quick to find whatever he needed and always discreet. Tonight she had been the very opposite: prickly, hostile, aggressive.

'Sorry, I'm just tired,' she said huskily. 'Thanks for the lift.'

She turned to get out of the car, but he caught her shoulder and spun her back towards him.

'Are you in love with Gilbey Collingwood?'

The curt question was like a slap in the face. She went white then red, and then rage exploded in her head and she hit him. Guy rocked backwards, letting go of her.

Sophie didn't waste time. She jumped out of the car without even looking, just as another car shot past them at high speed. There was a squeal of brakes, the rush of wind on her face, then something struck her shoulder and she was flung backwards, tumbling over the back of Guy's car into the road.

The other car slowed briefly, then drove on even faster, vanishing round the corner.

Guy got to Sophie before she had time to get up. He knelt beside her, his face pale in the lamplight. 'Sophie? Are you OK?'

She was still shaken by what had happened and could only mumble. 'I think so...'

'What in God's name happened?' asked Guy. 'I didn't see much, just heard him shoot past. Did he hit you? He didn't stop, the bastard, and he was going too fast for me to get his number in this bad light. Are you hurt?'

'Just my shoulder,' she said, rubbing it and wincing.

Guy gently explored, probing her whole shoulder area with gentle fingers, moving her arm up and down, watching her face for reaction. 'Does that hurt? This?' At last he said, 'I don't think you've broken any bones, but you may just have some bad bruising. I'll drive you straight to the nearest casualty department for an X-ray, though. It's best to make sure about these things.'

She stood up with his help, but shook her head. 'No, I'm too tired tonight. It doesn't hurt so much now, the pain's wearing off. If I have any problems I can always go to the hospital tomorrow.'

'Don't be stupid, Sophie!' he grated. 'It's wiser to go at once. You could have concussion; you must have hit that road at quite a speed.'

'I'm sure I don't have concussion. I took the fall on my side, not my head, and I don't have any symptoms except aching in my shoulder and a bit of a headache, which I had before that car hit me.' She gave him a polite smile. 'Goodnight, Guy, and thanks again. It's freezing out here. I want to get indoors.'

She made for the steps which led down to her basement. The street light didn't shine that far—the steps were in shadow, and slippery with ice and snow.

Hearing Guy behind her, she tried to hurry, to get away, which was a mistake; her feet skidded, and she clutched at the iron rail along the wall to save herself, dropping her handbag in the process.

It tumbled down to the bottom and sank out of sight into a white bank of snow which had blown down into the basement area and built up beside the wall of the house.

It seemed the last straw. Tears sprang into her eyes and she sobbed aloud. 'Oh, damnation and hell's bells!'

'This isn't your night, is it?' Guy drily said.

Luckily, that made her so angry that she brushed away the weak tears and snapped at him. 'I'm glad you find it so funny! The key to my flat is in that bag and now I've got to get my hands frozen, looking for it.'

He slid past her and kicked the snow, which flew everywhere in powdery showers. Guy bent and straightened again with her handbag in his hand, but, instead of giving it back to her, to her fury he actually opened it and looked inside.

'What do you think you're doing?' she demanded, outraged. 'Give it to me at once, and go away.'

He gave her a level stare which made her bite her lip, remembering belatedly that he was, after all, her boss. Not that that gave him any right to search her possessions, but she must remember to watch the way she talked to him.

'Please give me my bag,' she said carefully. 'Thanks for your help, but I can manage perfectly well now.'

'Oh, so far you've managed brilliantly,' he mocked. 'First you almost get run down, and then you tumble down these steps! If I didn't know you better, I'd think you were drunk.'

'Give me my bag!' Sophie said through her teeth, almost beyond caring now whether or not he gave her the sack.

He ignored her, fishing in her bag for her key, and, when he found it, turning to unlock the flat front door. He waved her through the open door and Sophie grimly limped through it, aching from head to foot, feeling faintly sick and a little giddy. Perhaps she had sustained some serious injury when she fell, after all? she thought. Wouldn't that be the perfect end to the perfect day?

Turning to block Guy's path, she tersely said, 'Goodnight,' holding out her hand for her bag and the key.

Guy did not give them to her. Instead, he came in with them and closed the door, with himself on the wrong side. Her side. She had wanted him on the other side; outside.

'Look, I'm very tired,' she said warily, watching him with barely concealed alarm. 'I'm really grateful to you for your help, but——'

'I think you need a strong brandy,' he interrupted.

She grimaced. 'I hate brandy.'

'It's good for shock,' he argued.

'Nonsense, it's very bad for it,' she said, sure she remembered hearing that. 'I'll make myself some hot chocolate, that's what I need, and I need rest. When you've gone...' She was beginning to get warning shivers down her back. How was she going to dislodge him and what exactly were his intentions in hanging on, refusing to leave?

She had never had this sort of trouble with Guy Faulkner before. He had always been a model boss: never a finger laid on her, no chasing around the desk or propositioning, always scrupulously courteous. Sophie had never felt nervous with him before but suddenly, looking up into his hard face, she felt a strange qualm of uncertainty. She had thought she knew him, but what was Guy Faulkner really like? And what would she do if he made a heavy pass at her late at night in her flat? He was thin, but she had a feeling he was strong, and she was feeling very weak.

'I asked you a question just before you got out of the car,' Guy said quietly. 'You didn't answer, which was answer enough, I suppose. You are, aren't you? In love with Gilbey Collingwood?'

She blinked, skin burning, hating him for persisting with the question. 'You're crazy...I...my feelings are nothing to do with you!' she stammered, and he gave her a crooked little smile.

'There you are wrong! It does have something to do with me. We're in the same boat.'

She stared, bewildered, and Guy sighed.

'Surely you knew I was dating Valerie until she suddenly dropped me for Collingwood?'

Her eyes rounded and her lips parted on a caught breath of surprise. She *had* forgotten that he had dated Valerie for a while. She certainly hadn't guessed he was serious about her, but then Guy Faulkner didn't give much away; he must be a great poker player.

'You were in love? I'm sorry, I'd no idea,' she said with husky sympathy.

He shrugged, his mouth reined in and angry. 'I'm glad to hear it. I try not to go around with my heart on my sleeve.'

'No, neither do I,' she said on a long sigh. 'In fact, I hate the idea of anyone knowing; that's why I didn't want to talk about it to you.'

'I realised that.' Guy gave her an unsmiling look, his eyes grave. 'As I said, we have a lot in common, including a dislike of talking about our feelings. I wouldn't talk to anyone else, but you and I can help each other.'

She gave him a puzzled frown. 'How?'

'By talking about it, to begin with...'

'About...them, you mean!' she muttered. 'No, Guy, I really don't want to. It's pointless.' Her voice rose shrilly, her mouth quivering, her eyes fever-bright. 'I just want to forget I ever met him, and talking won't help me do that. I was a crazy idiot to fall for someone like Gib, and the sooner I get over him, the better. So don't ask me to talk about him.' She looked at Guy and began to laugh wildly. 'But you don't want to talk about Gib, do you? You want to talk about her, that's all you're interested in...and I never want to hear her name again. Never again, do you hear? Never again.'

'Stop it! You're hysterical!' Guy bit out, taking hold of her shoulders and shaking her. 'And sit down, for heaven's sake, before you fall down. You're trembling like a leaf.'

She stopped laughing, and realised he was right, she was trembling and her teeth were chattering; with cold, or the shock of being hit by that car, or more probably with the mounting tension of this unending day.

She couldn't keep her tears back any longer, either. They came with the violence of a tropical storm and she covered her wet face, weeping angrily.

'Oh, go away, please...just leave me alone...I can't bear any more...I really can't...'

Guy put his arms around her again, as he had in the party, but this time he did not dance her around the room. He picked her up as if she were a child and carried her into her bedroom, laid her on the bed and sat down beside her, still holding her. Sophie cried helplessly, great, painful sobs which wrenched her like stabs of pain, her face buried against Guy's chest.

He stroked her hair and murmured wordlessly to her and gradually her sobs subsided; she had cried herself out. Guy's hand still moved in long, rippling strokes from the crown of her head, down her long golden-brown hair, which was flowing loose down her back. He must have undone the ring which held her chignon together, but she hadn't noticed him doing so. Now, he softly winnowed her hair with his long fingers, his touch warm and tender; and Sophie was hypnotised.

In a sort of trance, she lay against him with closed eyes, giving herself up to the sensual comfort, sighing with pleasure.

His hand slid down and began massaging her bruised shoulder, and she flinched away, afraid he would hurt her; but the touch was too gentle, avoiding the centre of the bruise, as if his fingertips were sensitised to her pain.

'If you won't go to the hospital, at least let me take a look, to make sure it isn't serious,' he murmured, and leaned over to switch on the bedside lamp.

Sophie blinked, blinded by the sudden light. 'No, it isn't serious,' she stammered, but Guy had already deftly unzipped her yellow dress at the back.

He drew it down off her shoulder and Sophie twisted to pull it up again.

'No, Guy!'

He caught her wrist and pushed her hand down firmly. 'It won't take a second and it will take a load off my mind to be sure you weren't badly hurt! Just keep still while I look at this.'

She sat still, her mouth mutinous. Guy stared at her bared shoulder, frowning.

'It's going to be all the colours of the rainbow!' he said wryly. 'Yes, it's a bad bruise. You should see a doctor, have something put on it.' He examined the area around the bruise, gently pressing down on her flesh, then said slowly, 'But luckily you escaped serious injury, unless there's something you aren't telling me.' His dark blue eyes probed her face. 'Is there?'

'No, I told you. A few bruises, that's all.' She was uneasy, sitting there with her dress half off and Guy staring at her. 'Can I zip my dress up again? You must go, Guy! I need to get some sleep!'

He caught hold of her chin and turned her face up towards him. Sophie's breathing stilled for a beat of time as she saw the look on his face. Guy bent forward and kissed her, and, although she had intended to push him away, her lips parted of their own volition. Some inner compulsion she hadn't reckoned with craved human warmth, to be touched, held, made to feel human again. She needed something to soothe the pain she had been carrying around all day.

Her hand went up and clasped his head, her eyes closed, and Guy sighed against her mouth.

'This is what you need,' Guy whispered. 'We both need it. Not sleep. You fight fire with fire, you burn it out, leave nothing but scorched earth behind. Help me to forget, and I'll help you, Sophie...'

It made some sort of crazy sense, and she felt her mind cloud with desire and grief and a longing for the oblivion he was offering. If she had had time to think she would have sent him away, refused. But she was at her lowest ebb, she was sad and lonely, and too weak to think clearly.

He sensed her submission, and reached over to switch off the bedside lamp again. In the darkness his mouth grew fiercer, hot and demanding, and she clung, kissing him back, her arms around his neck, holding his thick, dark hair and pulling him down against her, her slender body twisting against him.

Her dress slid further down, and Guy cupped her breasts with his hands, kissed their cool flesh, burrowed into the warm, soft valley between them, groaning, and suddenly Sophie's head cleared; she thought quickly and coldly of what she was doing and knew that she should stop him, now, before it was too late.

She couldn't deny she was tempted, though; and that was a shock in itself. She had never believed she would ever be tempted this way, but then she had never realised just how tempting sensuality could be when you were weakened by unhappiness and a yearning for something you could not have.

Guy's caressing hands and mouth sent shudders of pleasure through her whole body. Her flesh was so hot that she felt she was melting. But that cool, common-sense voice in her head wouldn't be quiet. Are you out of your skull? it nagged. You're really considering going to bed with a man you don't love, don't even know very well, and aren't one hundred per cent sure you like?

I want him, she argued back. Or, rather, I want this, this incredible feeling which is making my head swim and my mouth dry. Who's talking about love? Oh, I know I've never done anything like this before. I've always held back, determined to wait until I met someone I could love, but where has that got me? I was in love with Gib, and sure he was the lover I had waited for, and he's marrying someone else—a girl who had more boyfriends in a month than I've had in my whole life! While I was being sensible and waiting for Mr Right, Valerie Knight was having a wonderful time with every guy she fancied, and she still got Gib in the end!

Well, from now on I'm going to play the game her way, I'm going to enjoy myself in future, and I'm starting here and now, tonight.

Guy was kneeling above her, taking off his shirt. He had taken off her elegant yellow dress, her silky underwear; she was naked and Guy was staring down at her as he stripped, too. She could hear him breathing roughly, and Sophie trembled at being watched like that. She was excited and frightened, all at the same time, and, in an instinctive, female gesture, she drew her long golden-brown hair across her face, in a curtain, a veil to hide behind.

He laughed softly, huskily, as if the gesture delighted him, and then he came down to her, his warm, naked body heavy, his fingers drawing the curtain of her hair, his eyes gleaming at her in the darkness.

'You're beautiful,' he whispered, his voice shaking, and Sophie arched to meet his kiss.

Then the phone rang.

They both lay there, frozen, listening. 'Ignore it,' Guy said, but it had broken into Sophie's moment of madness, forcing her to wake up and think sanely. Her body was now as ice-cold as it had been burning hot.

'I can't,' she said wearily, putting out a hand to pick up the phone.

'I'll get rid of them!' Guy said fiercely, snatching the phone from her.

'No! Don't!' Sophie broke out. Whoever was on the other end of the line was going to be fascinated when they heard a man's voice, at this hour. What if it was Uncle Theo? He would be down the stairs and smashing down the basement door in no time. He had been protecting Sophie from the world since she was six years old, and especially from men.

'Hello, what do you want?' Guy was saying tersely. There was a pause, then he snapped, 'No, she's busy, she can't talk to anyone.'

'Who is it?' Sophie hissed, trying to take the phone from him, but as she did so his face and voice changed.

'What? Why? Who is this? Oh, Fabien, it's you.'

Sophie moaned in horror. 'Fabien?' The editor of the *Sentinel*? Guy's blue eyes flicked a glance at her, nodding a silent answer to her whispered question.

'Yes,' he said coolly into the phone. 'Yes, it is me. Clever of you to recognise my voice; I didn't recognise yours. Why have you been looking for me?'

Sophie pulled the brilliant patchwork quilt, which had been a present from an American cousin, from the floor, where it had fallen from the bed, and wrapped her shivering body into it while she listened. Guy switched on the bedside lamp and his hard face suddenly came into sight, giving her a strange shock, as if he had become a stranger, in the dark, while they were making love, and suddenly the familiar man was back.

'I see,' he said slowly. 'Yes, I think you may have a problem there. I'll come over to Barbary Wharf at once to go over it word by word.' Another pause, then he said flatly, 'That's OK. Sophie will understand. There are always other nights!'

Sophie flinched. She turned her head away, her face burning. Other nights? If he thought that, he was in for a shock. She had been acting like a crazy woman tonight, a blind and reckless fool; but her insanity was over.

'I'll be there in about twenty minutes,' Guy said, and hung up. He picked up his clothes and began dressing rapidly, and talked to her as he did so, his voice quiet.

'You heard all that. I have to go. I'm sorry, Sophie, I didn't expect him to recognise my voice.'

'Why did you take the phone away from me at all?' she bitterly reproached. 'Now he knows you were here . . . and . . . and you more or less told him what we were doing, and it will be all round Barbary Wharf!'

'Fabien won't gossip! He isn't some typist, he's the editor of a national newspaper, for God's sake!' Guy buttoned his shirt and began to put on his tie, facing her dressing-table mirror. She saw his reflected image, the tension of his bones, his straight, angry mouth, his eyes dark and impatient. 'Sophie, I'm sorry, you must know I didn't intend this to happen. He took me by surprise. He was ringing you because they've been trying to get in touch with me and couldn't trace me, and they thought you might know where I was tonight.'

'No doubt somebody saw us leave the party together, and passed the information on!' she flung at him.

'Possibly,' he admitted curtly. 'Anyway, Fabien is worried about a story that they're thinking of running as the front-page lead. It came in late, and hasn't been checked, but Fabien's afraid it could be libellous.'

'I thought you were off duty tonight. Isn't it Henry's turn to be the night lawyer? Why didn't they ring him?'

'That's the point,' he said soberly. 'Henry was whisked off to hospital from the office two hours ago.'

She was shocked by that news, her eyes widening. 'No? Oh, poor Henry—it isn't anything serious, is it?'

'Fabien thinks it might be that ulcer of his. We've all been laughing about it and teasing him, poor old guy, but apparently he really does have an ulcer and it could have perforated. They may operate tonight, it seems. We'll know more tomorrow.'

'Is a perforated ulcer very serious?' she asked, distracted from her own problems by thinking about Henry's. He could be pompous and patronising, but she was fond of him; he was almost like another uncle to her.

'It depends on how bad it is and whether or not they operate in time,' Guy said, looked at his watch and frowned. 'I must go, Sophie. The deadline for this edition is one a.m. and it's gone midnight now. I'll see you tomorrow.' He bent and kissed her quickly before she could turn her head, and then he was on his way to the door.

Sitting on the bed, wrapped in her quilt, only her face, framed in tousled brown hair, visible, she listened to his footsteps going away. The front door opened and closed quietly. Guy was so thoughtful. He had not forgotten the neighbours. He even drove away slowly until he was a little way down the street when she heard his car accelerate round the corner.

Sophie didn't move for a long time. Her body chilled, despite the warm quilt still clutched around her, she sat there, brooding.

Guy might claim that Fabien Arnaud would never stoop to gossiping, but Sophie knew how scandal got around at Barbary Wharf. Fabien had been talking on the phone from the office, hadn't he? He wouldn't have been alone. There would have been a whole night rota of staff within earshot: printers, journalists, secretaries. Not to mention telephonists. If Fabien had been looking for Guy, he would have gone through the switchboard for most of the calls, and the telephone girls were the worst gossips on the paper.

Within twenty-four hours it would be the talk of the *Sentinel* that she and her boss were sleeping together.

I'll have to resign, she thought. I can't bear being whispered about, having people stare, giggle. Having jokes made, hints dropped. And, even if the story didn't spread, if nobody but Fabien ever knew, she wasn't seeing Guy again. She couldn't even go on working for Guy after tonight. She never wanted to set eyes on him again.

CHAPTER TWO

SOPHIE hardly slept that night. She got up as soon as it was light, and left for work an hour earlier than usual. When she got to her office, she found a hurriedly scribbled note on her desk. Guy had not gone home until half-past one; he might be late that morning.

Well, that gave her even more time for what she meant to do! She had wanted a breathing-space without him around. She made herself a cup of strong coffee, and while she was drinking it typed out a brief letter of resignation, which she put on Guy's desk. She would be sorry to give up this job, sorry to leave the *Sentinel*, but she could not go on working with him after last night.

With a sigh, she began the usual routine of the day: consulting Guy's diary to see what appointments he had, getting out of the files any documents he would need to consult beforehand; reading through the post and sorting it into piles: urgent, important, non-urgent, and junk mail which could be consigned at once to the waste-paper basket.

But her nerves were on edge and every little sound made her jump about ten feet into the air.

At a quarter to ten the phone rang. it was Hazel van Leyden, asking for Guy.

'He isn't in yet—he worked very late last night,' Sophie said, hoping Hazel couldn't hear the shake in her voice.

'Of course he did, I'd forgotten. Look, Sophie, can you find the papers on the Cameron libel case and bring them up here? Mr Caspian wants to go through them again.'

'Yes, of course.'

Sophie knew exactly where the papers were—she had put them on Guy's desk so that he could refresh his memory of the details of the case, because that afternoon he would be seeing the barrister who would be representing the newspaper in court.

She was on her way towards the door with them when Guy walked in and both of them stopped dead. Sophie coloured painfully, and Guy gave her a shrewd, searching look. A wry smile curled his mouth.

'Good morning, Sophie. Sleep well? I didn't.' His voice lowered, intimate, mocking. 'Frustration kept me awake half the night.'

She caught back a cry of distress, but he heard it all the same, and registered it with a quick flick of those clever eyes. He didn't say anything, however, turning away to take off his thick overcoat and dark red wool scarf and hang them up.

'I have to take the Cameron papers up to Mr Caspian,' Sophie muttered, sliding past him while he had his back to her.

'Wait!' he said sharply and in spite of herself she halted, her nerves on edge. But all he said was, 'Tell him I'll need them back before lunch so that I can read them before I see Sir Charles Luther. I'll need to be needle-sharp with every tiny detail; he's a demon for accuracy.'

'Yes,' Sophie said, hurrying away, sighing with relief at the realisation that she wouldn't be in the same room when he read her letter.

She heard Gina Tyrrell laughing in Hazel van Leyden's office, but as she opened the door silence fell and both women looked round at her.

'Oh, hello, Sophie,' they said in unison.

Sophie stiffened, flushing, wondering if they had heard talk about her and Guy already. Was that what they had been laughing about? The very idea sent ice down her back.

'The Cameron case papers,' she muttered, averting her eyes from them. 'Can we have them back before midday, please? Mr Faulkner has to read them before he sees the barrister this afternoon.'

She put the bulky file on the desk and walked out without another word, although she was very conscious of the raised eyebrows and stares of the other two. As the door closed behind her Hazel said wryly, 'What's the matter with her this morning?'

'Maybe she has a headache? I expect she went to Valerie Knight's engagement party last night, and, if you remember, Sophie was mad about Gilbey Collingwood too. It can't have been easy for her to accept that he was marrying someone else.' Gina slid off the desk, her vivid russet hair gleaming in a brief shaft of wintry sunlight. She was wearing a jade-green wool dress which made her look even lovelier than usual, and Hazel watched her with envy, groaning aloud.

'You're so slim! When I think that six months ago I was as slim as that I could scream!' She looked down at her own thickening waist and grimaced.

Gina gave her a wry smile which held envy of a different kind. She often wished that she had had a child during her brief marriage to James Tyrrell, the grandson of Sir George Tyrrell, the previous proprietor of the *Sentinel*. But neither of them had been in a hurry to start a family; they had been very young and far too happy. If she had only glimpsed the future...but how could she have guessed that James would die so suddenly in a stupid, pointless accident?

'You can't have a baby without losing your figure,' she reminded Hazel. 'But never mind, only another four months to go!'

Hazel sighed. 'I know, but I seem to have been pregnant forever!'

'The baby's due at the end of April, isn't it?'

Hazel nodded. 'On the calendar it doesn't look long, but what they don't tell you is how time can drag when you're waiting; and what stupid little problems you come up against. My ankles are always swollen by the time I get home after work, and I can't run for a bus any more, or get into anything more glamorous than a tent!'

The intercom buzzed angrily and Nick Caspian's voice demanded, 'Where are those papers on the Cameron case?'

'I'm just bringing them,' Gina told him.

'Well, hurry up!' he snapped, then the intercom went dead again.

Gina pulled a face. 'He's another little ray of sunshine this morning.' She was too irritated by his snarls to rush in with the Cameron papers. Let him wait! Lingering, she said to Hazel, 'I gather there was trouble in the middle of the night over a front-page lead, and Fabien didn't ring Nick to tell him about it.'

'Well, I'm surprised Fabien didn't,' said Hazel, opening a filing cabinet and putting documents away into folders, talking over her shoulder. 'He should have done! He knows that anything at all dubious has to be referred to Nick first, to make sure there are no more lawsuits.'

'Well, he has this old-fashioned idea that the editor is the man responsible for what goes into his paper!'

Gina's dry tone made Hazel grin. 'Oh, of course, you're on Fabien's side against Nick Caspian!'

'I'm on the side of the *Sentinel*! I believe a newspaper should have a heart and conscience; not just be kept from publishing scandal and innuendo by the fear of libel suits. If Nick didn't encourage his reporters to write up the sort of stuff the *Sentinel* wouldn't have touched with a bargepole while the Tyrrells ran it, there wouldn't be any libel suits, and Nick wouldn't need to insist on the editor asking his permission for every story that goes in!' She gave Hazel a defiant look, her slanting green eyes bright with anger. 'So, yes, I am on Fabien's side, I suppose. Fabien's quite right to resent having his rights as an editor taken over by the proprietor. When Nick took over, he talked a lot about respecting editorial privilege, but he didn't mean a word of it.'

Hazel admired Gina's loyalty to her dead husband's family, and the ideals the Tyrrell family had stood for, but she wasn't sure she agreed with Gina's view of the changes in the *Sentinel* since Caspian International took control. Hazel secretly preferred the newspaper the way it was now: it was brighter, with more pictures, plenty of interesting features and some very readable columns from people like Valerie Knight, who was witty, acid and endlessly entertaining. Hazel had liked working for Sir George Tyrrell, but she had often found the *Sentinel* heavy going in his day.

Gina was watching her thoughtfully as she came back to her desk, but her mind had wandered from the subject of the *Sentinel*.

'Is Piet getting used to the idea of the baby?' she asked Hazel, whose face lit up.

'Yes, thank heavens. Remember how worried I was about telling him? And of course he was furious at first; he thought it was the end of his dream of starting our own design business. It took me ages to persuade him that we can still do that! We'll work something out: get an *au pair* or just take the baby to work with us. After all, we'll be the bosses! Once Piet accepted the idea of the baby, he got quite excited. I think it's because he can actually see I'm pregnant now.'

'Everyone can!' teased Gina and Hazel giggled, a hand on her bump.

'It is getting obvious, isn't it?'

Gina smiled back at her. 'You look wonderful.' Her eyes flicked to Nick's door. He hadn't come storming in to find out what was keeping her, as she had expected.

Hazel caught that glance and interpreted it correctly, grinning. 'Waiting for him to stampede in here? You do love to provoke the man, don't you? I'm almost sorry for him sometimes.'

'Don't be!' Gina muttered. 'He deserves everything he gets. But I'd better take this file in to him, I suppose!'

As she walked into his office she heard Nick laughing, and halted in surprise. A quarter of an hour ago he had been snarling with rage over Fabien Arnaud's failure to keep him informed. Now his hard eyes were alight with amusement, and his lean body had relaxed back against his swivel chair, that thick black hair of his touched with the odd strand of silver, which only showed in some lights.

The abrupt change of mood was typical of him. He was a mercurial man. Gina kept thinking she knew him, only to be utterly bewildered by some new shift in his mood, some new light on his character.

Still laughing, he turned and held out his hand for the Cameron file, but her delay had not, after all, escaped him. 'You took your time!' he accused. 'Gossiping with Hazel again, were you? Do you two ever get any work done?'

'I suppose you and Fabien were laughing your heads off over work when I came in?' she retorted.

Nick's grey eyes gleamed with wicked amusement. 'In a way. You know Fabien had to call Guy Faulkner last night because Henry Sandel had been taken ill? There was no reply from Guy's flat so Fabien rang the hotel and talked to someone at Valerie Knight's engagement party. Guy had been there, but he had left . . . and guess who with?'

Gina frowned, her mind busy. 'Not . . . Valerie?'

Nick's black brows shot up; he and Fabien exchanged glances. 'No,' Nick slowly said. 'Interesting you should jump to that conclusion, though. She and Guy dated before she started seeing Collingwood, didn't they? Don't you think it's past history, then?'

Gina shrugged and didn't answer.

Nick leaned back, studying her expression with interest. 'Barbary Wharf is a hive of intrigue, isn't it? I can see I miss out on a lot by having to leave London so often. But I do remember that Collingwood himself once dated Guy's cool-as-a-cucumber secretary. And that was who Guy left the party with—Sophie Watson! Presumably they were drowning their sorrows together. Fabien got hold of her address and telephone number, and rang, around midnight, and it was Guy who answered the phone. Fabien says he sounded distinctly dishevelled.'

'How can you *sound* dishevelled?' His amusement annoyed Gina. No wonder Sophie looked fraught this morning! Perhaps she realised that her private life was public property now? Gina sympathised. She knew that *Sentinel* staff talked about *her* behind her back and she resented it. It was like living in a goldfish bowl! From what she knew of Sophie Watson, she would hate that.

Fabien answered her, sounding very French and amused. 'Oh, but it was obvious, you know! He was so breathless that I could hardly make out a word he said, and his voice was low and husky. It was easy to guess what they had been doing when I rang!'

Fabien was actually Swiss, but came from a French-speaking canton of Switzerland, and had distinctly French tastes and attitudes, including a sophisticated view of adult relationships. He and Nick got on well, although Gina suspected that was because Fabien took care to disagree with Nick as little as possible. Smooth, discreet, clever, he reminded Gina of a sparrow: brown hair, brown eyes, neat and quick-footed, he darted around, picking up crumbs and managing to survive in difficult circumstances. So far there had never been a clash of deeply ingrained beliefs between the two men, but Gina lived in hope. Somewhere buried inside Fabien she hoped there was an editor with integrity. But at that moment she did not like Fabien very much at all.

'The only thing that is obvious is that you two have got nasty minds!' she snapped, eyeing Nick with a distaste that drove the smile from his face.

'Come on, Gina,' he retorted. 'What do you think they were doing alone in her flat, at that time of night? Playing Scrabble?'

'Talking, arguing, discussing politics—who knows or cares?' Gina said fiercely. 'Does sex have to be the answer to everything? Can't you imagine a man and woman having a platonic relationship?'

Nick laughed curtly. 'No, I can't! Not if they're under sixty, and, even then, I'd have my doubts! When an attractive man is alone with an attractive woman, he doesn't have his mind set on discussing politics!'

Her green eyes flashed. 'You mean *you* have a one-track mind where the opposite sex is concerned! You're only interested in a woman for one reason!' She saw his black brows jerk together in a heavy frown, but he wasn't intimidating her; she went on angrily, 'Thank heavens all men aren't like you! Guy drove his secretary home from an office party, late at night, so that she didn't need to get a taxi or risk public transport late at night! It was kind and considerate of him—and it doesn't have to mean any more than that.'

'Fine,' said Nick curtly. 'So why was he still there an hour later?'

'Maybe she invited him in for a cup of coffee? What's wrong with that? It doesn't mean anything else was on offer!' She deliberately looked away from him towards Fabien, her face grim. 'Sophie Watson is a nice girl, and if you spread this gossip around you could ruin her reputation and make her very unhappy. Is that what you want?'

'No, of course not,' he said quickly, and Gina would have been satisfied with that if she hadn't noticed Fabien's expression. Was that guilt she read in his eyes? Or just embarrassment? It suddenly occurred to her that he might have told others before telling Nick, but before she could ask any more questions Fabien looked at his watch, and said, 'I must go! I have a lot to do before the editorial conference this morning.'

He walked out and Nick glared at her, his eyes like knives. 'You just love to feel superior, don't you? Fabien didn't mean any harm, and he wasn't sitting in judgement on Guy or Sophie Watson. They're both free and they're both adults—nobody is going to be horrified if they have an affair. So get down from that high moral horse, will you, and join the real world?'

'You mean your world!' she threw back, her face flushed and furious. 'No, thanks, I'd rather jump out of that window!'

She walked away very fast, and Nick's glittering grey eyes watched the sway of her slim body angrily, with desire, with violence.

'One day, Gina,' he muttered. 'One day you'll go too far.'

'The further from you, the better!' she flung back before slamming the door behind her.

Hazel was talking on the phone; she turned to mouth, 'Philip Slade! Want to talk to him?' at Gina, who nodded a little reluctantly, taking the phone. She had dated Philip for a few months, but for a while now she had been trying to avoid him without offending him. She liked him as a friend, but Philip wanted more than friendship and she couldn't give it to him.

'Hello, Philip, how are you? I thought you were in the Bahamas!'

'I am! I'm ringing from Nassau, on New Providence...'

She sighed. 'Lucky you! And I suppose the weather is gorgeous, blue skies, sunshine... it's snowing here, by the way, and bitterly cold! So I shouldn't hurry home.'

He laughed. 'I wasn't going to!'

She heard another voice somewhere in the background, a high, birdlike voice with a note of complaint.

Philip murmured something aside. 'Yes, yes...' he said, and then spoke into the phone again. 'Gina, I'm ringing because... I've got something important to tell you...' His voice sounded uncertain, nervous. 'You see... well, the point is... I'm getting married!'

Her eyes widened. 'Philip!' She was startled by the suddenness of the news. She hadn't even known that he was seeing anyone else. 'Congratulations!' she added quickly, before he could start to wonder if she minded. She didn't—there was nothing of the dog in the manger about Gina—but she was stricken by the possible consequences for her of Philip's getting married. 'Who is she? Do I know her?'

'No, I met her out here. Just three weeks ago.' He laughed, sounding pleased with himself.

'Three weeks ago!'

'Yes, it all happened very fast, a real whirlwind romance. I've just telephoned an announcement to the *Sentinel* but I didn't want you to read it in the paper before I had a chance to tell you myself.'

'That's very sweet of you, and I hope you'll both be very happy; do give her my best wishes, won't you? Tell me about her—what's her name, where does she come from?'

'She's American, from California. Japanese American, actually; I can't pronounce her real name, but everyone calls her Suki, anyway, Suki Tamaki. She's beautiful and much cleverer than I am, Gina! She's a lawyer, but she works for her family—and guess what? The family are in the newspaper business, too. Isn't that a coincidence? I'm sure you're going to like her. I've told her about you, I explained that we were just friends now, and she's dying to meet you.'

Gina's brows lifted silently. Did he believe that? Probably. Philip had always had a low credulity threshold where women were concerned, especially if it suited him to believe what they told him.

'I'm dying to meet her, too,' she said.

'Thank you, Gina!' Philip sounded grateful and relieved. She might have stopped seeing him some months ago, but his ego probably made him think she would be jealous and angry when she heard he was marrying someone else. He wouldn't want to believe she didn't care. Happily, he said, 'I must go, Gina. See you when Suki and I get to London; we're coming for Christmas with my family.'

'Bye...' Gina said as he hung up, and then she put down the phone and turned to Hazel, who had shamelessly eavesdropped and was grinning.

'Did I gather he's met someone else?'

'Not just met! Got engaged to! He was ringing to warn me before I read it in the paper tomorrow. He says her name is Suki, she's American, of Japanese descent, and her family is in the newspaper business in California. I've got some vague memory of having heard about them, I think; I must ask Nick. He's bound to know all about them.' Gina sat down behind her desk and shook her head. 'I feel quite dazed after that.'

Frowning, Hazel tentatively asked, 'Do you mind? I mean . . . you and Philip were seeing a lot of each other at one time, weren't you?'

'Of course I don't mind. We were just good friends, and you can quote me if you're asked!' Gina grinned at her. 'No, I'm simply amazed by the speed of it. He only went to the Bahamas in the middle of November.'

'Love happens like that sometimes.' Hazel sighed, gazing into the distance with a dreamy expression in her eyes. 'I knew from the minute I met Piet that he was the guy I wanted, it really was love at first sight, although I didn't admit it to myself right away because I was so furious because he only looked at you, not me. It took a lot longer for Piet to fall in love with me!'

'He told me he fell in love with you when he saw you trip, and get up covered in white paint and mud, that day we came to look over Barbary Wharf together, for the first time,' Gina said, giggling.

Hazel could laugh about that now, although at the time it had made her angry enough to bite someone.

'Yes, Piet thought I was too perfect to live! He said I looked human for the first time when I fell on my face.'

'Men are weird, aren't they?' Gina stopped smiling, her green eyes sharp with anxious thought. 'I just wonder if getting married will make any difference to Philip's support for me? If he changes sides, or sells his shares to Nick, I'll never be able to block Nick in future when I disagree with what he's doing. It will give Nick full control on the board and on the paper. I've only managed to fight Nick because Philip's shares, added to mine, gave me an edge.'

She and Nick had been fighting for so long that it had become an addiction to her, a strange, heady excitement, like playing Russian roulette, knowing all the time that you walked the razor edge of destruction. She knew she couldn't ever win; he had too much power with the other members of the board, and however much she detested him she had to admit he was a brilliant newspaperman—he had amazing flair for the business, and quite often she was happy to support his plans.

But she couldn't bear to contemplate Nick winning, ending up with full control. She feared what he would then do to the *Sentinel*; the process he had already started would accelerate rapidly, and the newspaper would lose all credibility as a serious newspaper. Since Sir George Tyrrell had died, leaving her his shares, Philip Slade had thrown in his shares with hers so that she and Nick were evenly balanced, but if Nick got hold of those shares she would be merely another board member, without the power to influence policy.

Most of all, she hated the idea that she would never again experience the passion and adrenalin of her long duel with Nick.

Hazel grimaced. 'I hadn't thought of that, but I suppose you're right. Still, I don't see why Philip should want to sell just because he's getting married—or why he should start supporting Nick instead of you! I doubt if anything will change, so don't worry.' Then she laughed. 'I tell you what, though! There's never a dull moment around here, is there? A new crisis every couple of hours! Oh, I'm going to miss the place when I leave.'

'I shall miss you,' Gina said soberly. Hazel planned to leave the *Sentinel* the month before she had her baby. Piet van Leyden would be leaving Caspian International some time soon to set up his own business as a freelance design consultant in Europe. He had made many contacts through working for Nick Caspian, and he was a very talented architect—Gina was sure he would be successful; she wasn't worried that he and Hazel might starve! But she wished Piet were not quite so ambitious or that he did not plan to base his business outside the UK. It would mean that she and Hazel would see very little of each other in the future, and Gina hated change and loss, especially from her closest circle.

Sophie walked back into her office nervously, but was relieved to find it empty. Guy was in his own office; she heard his voice, talking to someone on the phone. She sat down behind her desk and stared blankly out of the window. The terms of her contract meant that she had to work out a month's notice, which meant another four weeks with Guy, facing him, day after day, with the memory of last night always between them. How was she going to stand it?

'Miles away?' said a voice beside her, and she started violently, going pale as she looked round, but it wasn't Guy, it was Tom Birny in a chunky fisherman's sweater knitted in cream wool, worn over well-washed old blue jeans.

'S-sorry, yes,' she stammered, pulling herself together. She hadn't even heard him come into the room! 'What can I do for you, Tom?'

'I have to see your chief to check over a story before it goes through!' he said, as always making her feel dwarfed by his size and powerful shoulders. He must be a formidable rugger player; he was built like a wall, massive and immovable. Yet he was very different in character: he reminded her of a puppy, blundering about, leaping and gambolling, all grins and wide, hopeful, appealing eyes.

Sophie could still hear Guy's clipped tones through his office door. 'He's on the phone at the moment. Take a seat and he should be free soon,' she told Tom, who happily sprawled his long body over her spare chair.

'Good party last night, wasn't it?' he said. 'We played a great joke on old Gib, but you missed it, leaving so early. I saw you go off with your chief. Didn't realise you were dating him.' He grinned at her ruefully. 'Won't pretend I'm not disappointed. Meant to ask you out, myself.'

'I'm not dating him!' Sophie was flushed again, and angry. You couldn't do anything without someone noticing, putting two and two together and making a hundred, then spreading it all round Barbary Wharf!

'No?' Tom stared, uncertain.

'He just drove me home because I felt ill!'

Tom's face lit up. 'Well, great! Then, are you free tonight? Barry Eagle is opening his nightclub... remember Barry?'

Vaguely, she knew the name. 'Wasn't he a pop star?'

'That's Barry! Used to come on stage wearing an eagle costume, then shed it when he got too hot; it was part of his act—underneath the feathers he was almost naked! You should have heard girls screaming every time he did it!' Tom laughed uproariously. 'Mind you, he was a terrible singer, but he caught on at first. He was at the top for a couple of years, then he slid down the charts, so he moved over into the other side of the music business, started his own record company, and proved he had a real ear for coming talent. I think he makes a lot of money now; that's why he's branching out by opening his own nightclub, as a showcase for his coming stars.'

'I'd have thought that was risky—you could lose a lot of money that way.'

'I doubt if Baz uses his own money! He'll have borrowed it. I don't say he's a crook, but he has crooked friends, who have money to invest. Let's say, money that doesn't show up in their accounts, money that needs laundering—and I don't think Baz is too particular about things like that.'

'Sounds charming!' Sophie said drily.

Tom grinned. 'Oh, Barry's OK. We lived in the same street, when we were kids, went to the same school. He doesn't have many scruples about money, but he can be quite decent in other ways.'

'Don't tell me! He's kind to his old mother!' mocked Sophie, and Tom laughed.

'Well, actually, he is! Honestly, though, compared to some of the guys I have to mix with in this job Barry's Snow White in person, let me tell you!'

Sophie watched him curiously, realising that he might not be quite as simple as he seemed on the surface. 'It must be dangerous at times, being a crime reporter. It sounds like a tough life; what on earth made you want to do it?'

'I didn't, I wanted to be a sports reporter when I started, but I was offered a crime reporter's job on my first paper because they had a good sports reporter. I decided to accept, thinking I'd be able to switch later, than I got hooked on the job. Sometimes you're bored out of your mind for a week, then suddenly a big story breaks and everything changes, you're running on adrenalin, high as a kite, and you know you'd never want to do any other job in the world——' He broke off, grimacing. 'Sorry, I'm boring you!'

'No, I'm fascinated!' she insisted. 'I love hearing other people talk about their work!'

'You're a wonderful listener. You should be a reporter yourself, you'd make a good one,' Tom said, gazing at her with those big, wide, apparently innocent eyes. 'Have you ever thought of switching to editorial?'

She was startled. 'It has crossed my mind,' she confessed, wondering how he had guessed. Working with Guy had taught her that it was always possible to switch from one career to another, and she didn't want to be a secretary all her life. Sophie was ambitious.

'I'm not surprised. Clever girl like you.' Tom gave her a persuasive smile. 'Look, come with me tonight, and tell me all about it, what you want and what you're doing to get it!'

She looked blankly at him. 'Go with you? Where?'

'To Baz's nightclub,' he reminded. 'The Blue Penguin, he's calling it—don't ask me why! He has a weird sense of humour. It's going to be a glittering affair. There's a terrific cabaret lined up. Baz knows a lot of stars who will come: pop stars, sports stars, actors, and a lot of business people with money who will go to meet all the stars. Come on, Sophie, you'd enjoy yourself, and I'll look out for you, don't worry, you'll be quite safe with me.'

Slowly, she said, 'It does sound like fun, Tom, but...' She wasn't attracted to nightclub life, in fact; but she was feeling even worse than she had felt last night, both restless and reckless, wanting something to happen, wanting to defy what fate was doing to her life.

'Don't say no!' he pleaded, taking her hands and squeezing them in his powerful fingers.

She looked into his eyes and couldn't help smiling. 'All right, I won't, she relented, and Tom beamed.

Then Guy's door began to open and she snatched her hands out of Tom's grasp, her nerves leaping as she felt Guy's hard eyes narrow on them both. Had he seen Tom holding her hands?

Unaware of any atmosphere, Tom turned round and got to his feet and gave the other man a polite smile. 'Sorry to bother you, Guy, but I just want to check out where I stand on a story for tomorrow's edition...'

With something of a shock Sophie suddenly realised that they were almost the same height, if not the same build. Guy did not have Tom's obvious muscle, his deep chest and breadth of shoulders, but there was something about him that Tom couldn't match: a threat, a sense of danger, in the tilt of his chin, a look in his eyes.

'I'm busy, but I can give you five minutes,' Guy said in chilly tones.

Tom walked past him into the further office, and Guy stared at Sophie, his blue eyes as sharp and vicious as knives.

'I'll talk to you later,' he said softly, and she felt her stomach sink. That was what she was afraid of!

The door shut, she sagged in her chair and somehow forced herself to get on with her work, although she was trembling and kept making mistakes.

Tom was out again ten minutes later. He paused to ask her, 'Tonight, then—I'll pick you up at around seven-thirty? We'll have dinner there. Evening dress, I'm afraid; it's going to be a very swish affair. What's your address?'

She scribbled it down on a piece of paper, her hands shaking because she was very aware of Guy standing behind him in the doorway.

'See you, then,' said Tom happily, taking it from her, and left, whistling. Sophie defiantly met Guy's hard stare.

'Dating Tom Birny? Now, I wonder why you're doing that,' he drawled. 'You never have before, have you?'

'He didn't ask before,' she lied, and saw his eyebrows lift.

'That isn't what I've heard. I heard he'd been chasing you for weeks without getting anywhere.'

'Well, I decided to go out with him, and it's none of your business!'

'If you want to date someone, does it have to be a great oaf like Birny? He's the male version of a bimbo! A body without a brain in it!'

'I notice you don't risk saying that when he's around!' Sophie snapped at him.

Guy gave her a dry look. 'If I did, he'd probably take it as a compliment, or a joke, and laugh!'

'You mean, Tom is better mannered than you are—and better tempered, too!' she retorted. 'Well, I like him—so don't patronise him when I'm around!'

'Which brings us to the subject of your letter of resignation,' Guy bit out curtly.

She tensed, her chin lifting, as Guy drew her letter out
of his jacket pocket and, to her stunned disbelief, slowly
began tearing it up.

'I don't accept it!' he coolly told her, throwing the
pieces into her waste-paper basket.

'I'll type it out again!' Trembling, Sophie picked up
the basket and began gathering up the pieces.

'I'll tear it up again!' promised Guy.

Almost blind with rage, she glared at him, then, on
a wild impulse, lifted the basket and jammed it down
over his head.

Guy staggered back a pace, blundering into a metal
filing cabinet. She heard him swearing inside the basket,
then he pulled the thing off and dropped it on the floor,
spilling paper in all directions, while he came towards
her, his face dark with angry blood and his eyes
dangerous.

Terrified, Sophie backed and almost sobbed, 'Don't
touch me!'

Guy halted, staring down at her, his eyes searching
her face. 'What the hell is the matter with you?'

She couldn't answer, shivering against the wall, her
amber eyes enormous in her white face, but the way she
looked changed Guy's expression, made his face tighten,
the rage leave his hard eyes.

'Calm down,' he said quietly. 'I don't know what you
thought I might do to you, but you're perfectly safe.
I'm not dangerous. Sit down, Sophie, and let's talk sen-
sibly about this...'

She edged sideways slowly and collapsed into her chair,
gripping the desk with both hands, her knuckles white.

Guy walked over to the window and looked out at the
leaden winter sky. She watched his back, the long, lean
body under that elegant suit, the way his dark hair curled
in above his stiff white collar. He might be calmer now,
but that didn't make her feel any happier. After last night

she was always going to be physically aware of him whenever they were in the same room.

Without turning round he said, 'Now, what is this all about? Last night? Why not talk about it, instead of just handing in your notice and running away?'

She ran her tongue tip over her dry lips, and swallowed; but her voice still came out rustily, in a hoarse whisper. 'I ... can't ... it's too ...'

'Too what? Embarrassing?'

'Yes,' she whispered.

'Do you think I don't know you've changed your mind since last night? I knew first thing this morning when I saw your face as I walked into the office. Last night you were unhappy and I was there, and we started something that worries you now it's broad daylight. That's how it is, isn't it?'

She shuddered, and he turned then, as if picking up her response, and looked across the room at her.

'You see? I do understand. I realise you aren't the type that sleeps around. It may surprise you to hear that I'm not, either. Last night was a bad time for both of us, we'd both had a few drinks and we just grabbed at a little comfort, that's all. It isn't the end of the world.'

Sophie risked a look at his face, through her lowered lashes. He was watching her in his turn, but she couldn't read his expression. Guy was a lawyer, trained to persuade, to convince, to lie! How could she guess whether or not he meant what he said?

Quietly, he said, 'I suggest we put last night behind us and forget it ever happened. It was a mistake, and it won't happen again. I don't want to lose the best secretary I've ever had, and I don't think you want to stop working here, either, especially as you don't have another job to go to—do you?'

She shook her head, not meeting his eyes.

'Then what do you say?' he persisted, and she sighed.

'Yes,' she plunged on impulse. 'OK.'

'You withdraw your notice?'

She nodded; she did not want to leave the *Sentinel* or the legal department. If Guy kept his word and forgot about last night maybe they could go back to the way it had been until last night. But was it possible for either of them to forget?

CHAPTER THREE

As Sophie and Tom Birny arrived at the nightclub, in a taxi, they found themselves in a long queue. A stream of cars were pulling up and disgorging their passengers, men in evening dress, women in low-cut dresses, hurrying in to the club out of the snowy night. Overhead glittered a neon sign of a large blue penguin and even from the end of the West End street they could hear the heavy beat of a rock band·inside.

As their taxi waited Sophie suddenly leaned forward, her eyes wide. 'There's Gina Tyrrell!'

'Where? Going in to the club?' Tom craned forward, too.

'She just went inside,' Sophie said in an odd voice.

'Sure it was her?' Tom turned back to study Sophie's face. She grimaced at him.

'Certain! And you'll never guess who she was with!'

'Philip Slade?' Tom was always behind with office gossip and didn't know that Gina was no longer seeing the director whose name had been coupled with hers for months.

Sophie shook her head, her mouth wry. 'Mac Cameron!' She watched Tom's eyes open, his jaw drop.

'You're kidding!'

Their taxi moved on and stopped outside the entrance. The club commissionaire opened the door for them and gave Sophie his hand to help her alight. Sophie looked along the red carpet laid from the kerb to the club portals and couldn't help giggling.

'Now I know how royalty feels!'

Tom crooked his arm. 'Well, come on, Princess, let's mingle with the rich and famous!'

They were politely asked for their invitation card before they entered the club, then bowed inside, where they were met by Barry Eagle in a white evening suit which he wore with a black shirt and a gold lamé bowtie. Sophie bit her lip at the sight of him. Well, I suppose we're lucky he isn't dressed as an eagle, she thought.

'Hi, Tom!' he drawled, punching him in a friendly way. 'How's tricks?'

'Not too bad, Baz. You look pretty good yourself.'

Barry Eagle smirked complacently.

'The club looks terrific, too!' Tom added. 'I don't need a crystal ball to see that the Blue Penguin's going to be a huge success.'

'You betcha! I've spent months planning this! You're going to lose count of the famous faces you see, and it will be a media blitz for the rest of the week—every paper in Fleet Street sent someone.'

Were they all crime writers, though? wondered Sophie wickedly, and as if he picked up her thoughts Barry Eagle's rather treacly brown eyes flicked round to her. He looked her up and down, raked back his floppy dyed blond hair, and gave her what he obviously considered to be an alluring smile. 'Where have you been hiding all my life?'

For Tom's sake, she swallowed a sarcastic retort. Instead, she ran her hand through Tom's arm and leaned on him, fluttering her lashes and giggling.

Tom quickly said, 'This is Sophie.'

Barry Eagle smirked, ready to believe he was irresistible, took her hand and kissed it with a long, lingering look into her eyes. 'Well, hello, beautiful! Any time you get tired of old Tom here, let me know.'

Sophie smiled coldly, wondering if the faint bulge in one side of his white jacket was a gun. Or was her imagination running away with her because Tom had said Barry Eagle had criminal friends?

There was a rather sinister-looking man heading towards them now, for instance—he was a criminal type if ever Sophie had seen one. Barry Eagle's eyes followed hers.

'Oh, hello, Baines—everything OK?'

'I'm sorry to interrupt, sir, but we have a little problem with the champagne...' The other man respectfully intoned and Sophie bit her lip, trying not to laugh as she realised that he was the wine waiter.

'I knew we hadn't ordered enough, didn't I say so, Baines?' Barry Eagle muttered irritably, then gave Tom and Sophie a brief grimace. 'Sorry, problems! Excuse me, will you?'

'Baz is OK, really, just shows off a bit,' said Tom to her as they sat down at the table to which they were directed a moment later.

Sophie was staring round the room, and nodded. The room wasn't large, although it looked enormous because the ceiling and walls were covered in mirrors. The effect of all those reflections flashing back and forth was to disorientate you: Sophie felt quite unreal already. Revolving globes of coloured light hung high above the parquet dance-floor, on which a number of people were dancing at that moment, to a disco beat.

Gina Tyrrell, naturally, sat close to the dance-floor. Her table held seven other people; Sophie recognised several faces, including that of a member of the *Sentinel* board of directors; she didn't remember his name but she had seen him several times before.

Tom hissed at her, 'Hey, look! That *is* Mac Cameron with Gina Tyrrell! You were right!'

Sophie nodded, watching the other table through her lashes while she played with her glass of champagne. What on earth was Gina up to?

Back in the summer, the *Sentinel* had printed an interview between Valerie Knight and a young girl called Molly Green, who claimed that the famous actor, Mac Cameron, had been her lover and was the father of a baby she was expecting. Mac Cameron had angrily denied it, and was suing the paper for libel.

Sophie had typed the brief which the legal department had drawn up for the barrister conducting the *Sentinel* defence. They were, naturally, claiming that they were justified in what they had printed because it was the truth. Molly Green still insisted that Mac was the father of the child, which had been born back in September. A blood-test had been taken from the baby girl, but as yet Mac Cameron had not taken a blood-test himself, so far as they knew.

Sophie remembered rumours that Gina Tyrrell was dating Mac Cameron, back in the summer. Gossip had it that Nick Caspian had ordered her to stop seeing the actor, yet here they were together tonight. And with so many reporters in the club there was little chance they wouldn't be noticed! There would be a terrifying re-action from Nick if somebody printed a story about them.

She watched a photographer prowling through the tables, taking quick flashlit snaps of famous faces, and hoped he wouldn't include Gina in any of his pictures.

Somebody halted at their table at that moment and she looked up at a dark, olive-skinned man in faultlessly tailored evening dress. He gave Tom a nod. 'Hello, Birny, on duty or is this social?' His voice was deep, gravelly.

'I shall probably write a piece on the club,' Tom said, without warmth; he had stiffened oddly. Sophie sensed he did not like this man and she gave the stranger a closer look, frowning.

He stared back at her, his black eyes making her very nervous. He was handsome in a sculptured fashion, his face perfectly modelled, his black hair brushed flat.

'Introduce us, Birny,' he ordered, and Tom stammered as he obeyed.

'Sophie . . . Andreas Kirk.'

The dark man was still watching her; he suddenly smiled, surprising her with a charm she had not expected from those rather cold features.

'Sophie...a lovely name and it suits you!' He held out his hand, and she slowly held out her own; he lifted it to his lips in a graceful gesture. The brush of his mouth sent a shiver down her back; she snatched her hand away a second later and caught the amusement in his eyes.

'Are you a model, or an actress, Sophie?' he drawled. 'You have to be one or the other, with those looks and your flair for clothes...' His dark eyes wandered over her chignon of smooth golden-brown hair, the oval of her face, her bared white shoulders and low neckline, the figure-hugging peacock-blue of her dress.

'I'm a secretary,' Sophie said shortly, flushing under that sensual exploration. The way he looked at her made the hair stand up on the back of her neck.

'Sophie works on the *Sentinel*,' Tom told him. 'In the legal department.'

Andreas Kirk's fine dark brows lifted. 'Really?' His eyes stayed on Sophie, their gaze even more intense now. 'Do you like the job? You don't find the law boring?'

'No, I find it fascinating!' she coldly told him, re-senting the question.

'I wish you worked for me, then,' he drawled. 'Tom didn't mention it, but I'm a lawyer myself.'

She was startled into a gasp. 'A lawyer?' She had half decided that he must be one of Barry Eagle's rich crim-inal friends! He smiled sardonically, as if he could read her thoughts.

'A barrister, to be precise,' he nodded. 'And I can never get a good secretary who understands legal terms or has any interest in the law, unless she looks like the back of a bus. If you ever feel like a change, give me a ring.' He slid a hand inside his evening jacket, and, like a conjuror producing a rabbit from a hat, pulled out a business card.

As Sophie reluctantly accepted it, a flashlight ex-ploded near by and she looked up, startled. Andreas Kirk spun on his heel, blackly frowning, but the photographer had his back to them now, and was taking pictures of another table altogether.

'Did he take a picture of us?' Andreas Kirk curtly asked Tom, who gave a blank shrug.

'I didn't notice if he did. But somebody is waving to you from a table over there...'

Andreas Kirk shot a look in the direction Tom pointed out, and waved back at a woman in a poppy-red dress.

'I must rejoin my party, I'm afraid,' he murmured, his mouth crooked. 'But I hope you'll dance with me later, Sophie?' He didn't wait for an answer, just turned away calmly, apparently certain she would say yes.

As he walked away, Tom let out a groan. 'I thought he'd never go! I hope you didn't mind meeting him, Sophie. I'd no real choice...'

Sophie slowly detached her eyes from Andreas Kirk and looked at Tom. 'He's rather scary! I nearly fell through the floor when he said he was a lawyer!'

Looking surprised, Tom whispered, 'You mean you really didn't know who he was? He's famous, Sophie; he made his name defending some of the biggest villains in London, and he has some very dodgy friends! I've been to trials where he's made mincemeat of evidence you would have thought was solid concrete! The man is terrifying in a courtroom.'

'He's terrifying everywhere, I should imagine,' Sophie said, her eyes on Andreas Kirk as he sat down at a table close to the dance-floor. The blonde in the poppy-red dress put a possessive hand on his arm, fluttering her lashes.

Tom followed her gaze and laughed shortly. 'Poor old Baz is scared stiff of him, anyway. You can tell his status in Baz's book by where he's sitting. Right next to Mac Cameron's table!' He stared at the famous actor a little enviously. 'What do women see in Cameron? Do *you* think he's sexy? Can't see it, myself!'

'You're not a woman,' said Sophie. 'He's very sexy, believe me!'

Gina Tyrrell was thinking exactly the same thing as she listened to Mac Cameron amusing the whole table with a brilliant imitation of one of the theatre's most famous names. She watched his supple body moving; felt that amazing presence, the hooded blue eyes and quick, alive smile, and a little quiver of sexual attraction ran through her.

He is so sexy! she thought. She had not seen him for months, and had almost forgotten just how sexy he was! So far tonight he had barely looked at her. She could tell that he had been astonished, if not very angry, to see her with Sir Dermot, just as she, herself, had been taken aback to find out that he was one of their party tonight.

Sir Dermot Gaskell, playing one of his elaborate games again! She would have to have words with him later! What exactly was his motive in setting them up like this, anyway?

Across the table Sir Dermot met her eyes and she gave him a cool look. He smiled blandly back, unworried. Sir Dermot had been Sir George Tyrrell's godson and was still loyal to the old man's memory; he had resigned in protest when Nick took over but had recently been asked to come back on the board. When Nick told her that Sir Dermot was being brought back on to the board of directors, she had queried the wisdom of the decision, and Nick had shrugged and reminded her that Sir Dermot had many friends on the board, one of whom had been the intermediary between him and Nick. Sir Dermot wanted to mend the breach between them, he said; and Nick was convinced that Dermot was prepared to forgive and forget, but Gina wondered now if Nick, for once in his life, had made a stupid mistake and invited an enemy into his camp.

'Enjoying yourself, Gina?' Dermot broke into her thoughts, leaning towards her, his blue eyes bright with mischief and amusement.

He was tall and spare, in his fifties, with thick grey hair, but gave the impression of youth, perhaps because he kept his mind young by being open to new ideas all the time. One of his hobbies was investing in the theatre, which was how he came to be friendly with so many actors.

'What are you plotting, Dermot?' she murmured, and he grinned.

'Plotting? Who, me?'

'Yes, you!' She lowered her voice, almost whispering, 'You didn't tell me Mac Cameron would be here tonight, for a start!'

'Didn't I?'

'You know you didn't. Don't forget that you're back on the *Sentinel* board, Dermot, will you? You have a loyalty to the newspaper——'

'Have *you* forgotten where *your* loyalties lie, Gina?' Dermot interrupted and she stiffened, paling.

'Of course not, but——'

'You can't be on both sides at once. Either you're on Nick Caspian's side, or you're still a Tyrrell, and you fight him.'

'I do, I am,' she stammered, yet she felt guilt weakening her because she knew that as the months had gone by she had gradually, inch by inch, given ground in her fight against Nick. Oh, she still argued with him whenever it seemed to her that he was taking the *Sentinel* in a direction she felt was contrary to the Tyrrell way of doing things, but on a personal level Nick was always the victor.

She saw him every day at work, if he was in London, and sometimes he even talked her into going with him to international conferences, to the newspaper group's base in Luxembourg; she saw him at home all too often because he had bought the flat next to hers on the penthouse floor of her apartment block. They had lunch and dinner together all the time, always as representatives of the *Sentinel*, and always in other company. Those oc-

casions weren't private, weren't dates; yet she knew that
Nick constantly forced an intimacy on her which was
becoming a habit. She was no longer resisting him with
the same bitterness. He was insidiously taking over her
entire life.

'I hope you mean that, Gina, because one day you
may have to prove it,' Sir Dermot said, and she frowned,
staring uncertainly.

'What does that mean?'

Before he could answer, there was a roll of drums and
the lights went down amid a hushed murmur of excitement. A spotlight appeared, and in its blue circle
stood Barry Eagle.

He was flushed and slightly tipsy. He made a rather
confused speech, welcoming them all, then began
thanking his 'dear friends' for their support for his new
venture. He named the more famous among them,
another blue spotlight travelling around the room as he
did so, picking out those whose names he mentioned,
while a ripple of applause followed.

At last, Barry moved on to introduce the first act in
the cabaret, one of the more popular groups his company
recorded, playing their latest hit.

'You can bet he isn't paying them, and they can't
complain because on a night like this, with the audience
full of the media, they're getting free publicity for their
new LP!' Mac Cameron drily said to nobody in
particular.

'Cynical, but no doubt very true!' Sir Dermot laughed,
but after that nobody spoke because the music was so
loud that you couldn't hear yourself think, let alone talk.

During the cabaret Gina kept feeling that Mac
Cameron was watching her, but whenever she looked
towards him his eyes were fixed on the performance, and
he was frowning. She picked up angry vibes from him.
He had not been pleased to see her here tonight. Mac
was a good actor, but she didn't believe he was acting
his suspicion and anger. She was certain he had been

amazed when he'd first seen her tonight. The look on his face had been far too convincing. Whatever Sir Dermot was up to, Mac was not part of the conspiracy.

Everyone clapped and whistled with enthusiasm when the cabaret ended, then Barry Eagle himself came back to act as disc jockey so that people could dance. It gave Gina a shock when Mac stood up and held out his hand to her, silently, his hooded blue eyes compelling.

Gina couldn't refuse in public to dance with him; flushed and confused, she followed him on to the dance-floor without a word.

As they began to dance, Mac said in a low, harsh voice, 'What's going on Gina?'

She didn't pretend not to understand him. 'I have no idea. Sir Dermot rang and invited me to come tonight, but he didn't tell me you would be one of the party, too.'

His eyes searched her face; he was scowling like a sulky little boy. 'Is that the truth?'

She held his gaze, nodding. 'I don't doubt Sir Dermot is up to something, I knew he was as soon as I set eyes on you, but, whatever it is, I'm not in on the plan.'

He relaxed, gave a little sigh. 'Well, I'm glad about that, Gina!'

They danced in harmony for a few moments, then Gina said, 'I hear you're making a new film. Is it going well?'

He smiled down at her, charm in his face. 'I hope so, but you can never tell about any work until it's finished and you can stand back and see it clearly. What about you? How are you getting on with Nick Caspian now?'

'I suppose you can get used to working with the devil, if you have to!' Gina said and Mac broke out into deep laughter, his head thrown back.

A flashbulb exploded near by and they both looked round, startled. Gina groaned as a photographer grinned and said, 'Thanks, Mr Cameron; Mrs Tyrrell!' before moving on to take a picture of another of the dancing couples.

'Oh, not again!' Gina muttered, realising what was going to happen next day when Nick saw that picture in some paper or another.

'It was to be expected,' Mac drily pointed out. 'No doubt it was just what Sir Dermot wanted to happen!'

'Yes, of course it was—but why? What is he up to?' Gina wished she knew what serpentine manoeuvre Sir Dermot planned—what did he have to gain by publicly throwing her and Mac together again? It couldn't be just to annoy Nick. She sensed that something more was behind all this—why else had Sir Dermot said to her that one day she would have to prove her loyalty to the Tyrrell family?

There was some sort of conspiracy afoot, and Sir Dermot was hoping to lure her, or trap her, into becoming part of it. But where did Mac Cameron fit into that? She was sure he knew no more about it than she did—so how did Sir Dermot plan to use him?

'God knows what he's up to,' Mac said, swinging her through the other couples, towards the exit. 'But whatever it is, I'm leaving now—how about you?'

Gina didn't have time to think it through. On impulse, she decided to go, to walk out on Sir Dermot without another word. It served him right! He had no business using her in his private war with Nick without even telling her what was going on.

She had to collect her coat from the cloakroom, and when she returned found Mac, in a handsome black wool overcoat, talking on the club telephone.

'My car will be outside by the time we get there,' he told her, replacing the phone. 'I just talked to my driver on the car phone. He managed to find a parking space just around the corner and he's on his way to pick up up now.'

'But you came with us!'

'Yes, but I'd ordered my car to get here at eleven. I have to be at the studio at crack of dawn, and I can't afford to stay up late.'

As he predicted, his limousine pulled up as they emerged and the driver shot round to open the door for them and see them seated.

'We'll take Mrs Tyrrell home first,' Mac told the man. 'What's the address, Gina?'

'Are you sure? I mean, if you have to get up early... I can take a taxi, you know.'

'As I recall it, you live down by the river, not far from Barbary Wharf, so it isn't out of my way. I'm living in a riverside house I'm renting from a friend for six months, not far from the Tower of London.'

'Well, thanks!' Gina gave the driver her address and the car moved smoothly off. 'Do you like living by the river?' she asked.

'It's terrific in the early mornings, when there's mist, and you see the sun coming up through it, like a blood orange—or these morning, with snow around, the trees look like etchings——'

He broke off, then said almost shyly, 'Sorry to turn poetic—I get carried away when I talk about it. I just love watching the river while I have my first coffee of the day.'

'So do I,' she confessed. 'You don't need to apologise to me, I feel the same. I like to breakfast out on my balcony looking over the river.'

'Me too. Well, I don't eat breakfast, I just drink a coffee and some orange juice, if there's time before the car arrives to take me to the studio, to get made-up.'

'Which do you find easiest, films or the theatre?'

'Oh, films,' he said. 'You do scenes in easy bits, you don't have to learn the whole play by heart and be ready to perform it all every night. You never use up as much adrenalin doing a day's filming as you do every night of a theatre run. I used to come off stage drenched in sweat and shaking like a leaf, too hyper to come down easily, so I had to go out every night after a performance and bring myself down to earth slowly.'

'I remember,' she said, and their eyes met and held. It had been after a stage performance that Sir Dermot had introduced her to Mac the first time. Mac had asked her to join him for supper, to help him come down from that peak of intense excitement, they had talked easily together and she had liked him very much, but that night Mac hadn't realised who she was or known about her connection with the *Sentinel*. When he discovered the truth, next day, he had been so angry that he had told her he never wanted to see her again.

He was remembering all that, too, and grimacing. 'I'm sorry I acted the way I did, Gina. It was childish of me to be so angry with you, but I felt——'

'You thought I'd been underhand,' she said quickly. 'I hadn't intended to be, Mac. I was curious and then when I realised you had no idea who I was I was reluctant to tell you and spoil our evening. I would have explained later, if you hadn't found out first.'

A photographer had snatched a picture of them; it had appeared in a rival newspaper next morning. Nick had been violently angry when he saw it, and so, ironically, had Mac; each of them feeling betrayed.

'Sir Dermot fixed that, too!' Mac thought aloud, grimly.

'Yes,' she agreed, equally grim as she recalled how badly she had felt, and how impossible it had been to get either man to listen to the truth.

'I wonder what devious plan he has this time?' Mac considered, brow furrowed.

Gina shrugged. 'Whatever it is, Nick Caspian is the target. Sir Dermot is always looking for ways of hurting Nick and he'll use anyone as a weapon.'

'And he's using me because I'm suing the *Sentinel*,' Mac worked out aloud, his brows knit.

'And you can hurt Nick financially,' ended Gina.

'Oh, I hope so!' Mac muttered through his teeth.

Gina hesitated, afraid to reawaken his hostility towards her, but in the end deciding to risk asking a question which had been on her mind all evening. 'Did you see the pictures of the baby we published a few weeks ago?'

Mac stiffened. He didn't ask which baby she meant— he knew at once, turning his head away without replying at all, his eyes fixed on darkness.

Gina knew he was making it clear that he didn't want to discuss the matter, but she stubbornly went on, 'You did know that the hospital kept her in an incubator for a while because she was so small when she was born? She's doing very well now, though. She's so pretty, she has lots of curly dark hair, like her mother's, and blue eyes, but of course babies always have blue eyes at first, don't they? Molly has called her Deirdre—isn't that an unusual name?'

'It was my mother's name!' Mac burst out, his voice hoarsened with anger. 'She had no right...' He stopped, swallowing, his averted face taut and white.

Distressed, Gina said, 'I'm sorry, Mac, I had no idea! But...look, I know you're going to suspect my motives in saying this but...well...are you sure you aren't——?'

'The father?' he snapped. 'Yes, I'm one hundred per cent certain!'

Gina bit her lip, sighing. 'Oh. I don't understand it, Molly seems such a nice girl, and she's just as unhappy about all this as you are. I've met her several times now, and I could swear she was as honest as the day is long.'

'I thought so, too, once!' The bitterness in Mac's voice was just as genuine as the sadness in Molly's eyes, and it left Gina totally puzzled and confused. Which of them was lying? One of them had to be!

'You never slept with her, even once?' she persisted, and Mac shot her a narrow look, his face hostile.

'Are you sure it was Sir Dermot who set up this meeting? If you're here to pry, on behalf of Caspian——'

'I'm not! I give you my word, I'm not. It's just that I like Molly Green very much. I can't believe that she's lying...'

'So you think I am! Well, thanks very much!'

'No, Mac, I don't think you're lying.' Gina put a hand on his arm, her big green eyes pleading with him. 'Honestly, I don't, Mac. It's just that if you were never her lover...'

'I didn't say that!' he said in such low tones that she only just heard them.

Gina stared. 'What? But...'

Flatly, he went on, 'I said I can't be the father of the child; I know it's impossible.'

Slowly, Gina said, 'Are you saying that you did sleep with Molly? But, then...Mac, whatever precautions you took, you could still be the father——'

'No!' he snarled. He took a deep breath then said in a rush, 'I can't...I can't father a child!'

Gina stared at him, stunned into silence.

'Satisfied?' Mac hurled at her, his voice trembling. 'I was hoping it would never have to come out. It's going to wreck my life when everyone knows. I'm coming up to forty now, anyway; my days as a sex symbol are almost gone, and this will finish them altogether. Nobody will give me a leading role in a film again. I'll be a laughing-stock. I hoped Caspian would settle out of court.'

Gina said incredulously, 'Then why threaten a lawsuit in the first place?'

He gave her a bitter look. 'I wasn't letting her tell lies about me in print! And don't think I can't prove my story, if I have to—because I can, you can tell him that! I'll be bringing experts, I shall set up new tests before the case comes to court, but I've had them all in the past.' He laughed hoarsely. 'My God, believe me, I had every test available.'

Gently, Gina asked, 'When was this? I mean, why did you have these tests? What made you suspect that you...?'

'I was living with someone who wanted a baby, we'd tried for a couple of years, but she never got pregnant, so we both had tests, and they said it was me, they said I couldn't——' He broke off, then added bitterly, 'She left me. We'd been talking of getting married, but when she knew I couldn't have a child she walked out the very next day. Suddenly I was no good to her, she said she had to have a real man, one who could give her a baby.'

Gina shuddered. 'My God! How could she be so cruel?'

'At least she was honest, even if it hurt,' Mac grated. 'Molly looked like an angel, I was head over heels in love with her...'

Gina's green eyes widened and she stared harder at him, listening intently. So he had been in love with Molly, after all?

'But,' Mac went on fiercely, 'she turned out to be the biggest liar unhung! Now you see why I was so angry when she tried to make me believe I was her baby's father. I desperately wish it were true, heaven alone knows—I'd have given anything——' He broke off, his face working. 'But I knew it couldn't be mine, and I wouldn't let her tell lies about something that matters so much to me.'

Gina couldn't get to sleep for ages that night; she kept thinking about the pain in Mac's voice and face. There was no doubt about his sincerity. He was too unhappy to be lying, and yet... Gina had been just as convinced by Molly Green. They couldn't both be telling the truth, though. Could they?

She fell asleep at around one but woke up with a terrible, grinding shock as someone began ringing her front doorbell with angry insistence.

Gina knew who it had to be, of course. Only one man could get up here, to the penthouse floor of the apartment block. The whole floor was only to be reached by using an electronic code tapped into the lift computer in conjunction with a key which had to be inserted first.

She could even guess why he was ringing her doorbell at this hour. Nick must have seen the first edition of whichever paper had got that photo, of her and Mac Cameron, in it.

He would be furious with her, and she couldn't blame him. That picture could make it look as if she was on Mac's side in the court case; Nick had every reason to be angry, but she was too tired to cope with a row with him tonight. She was tempted to ignore the ringing until he went away, but Nick was persistent; he simply put his thumb on the bell and kept it there, and the noise split her head with pain, so, dazed and a little shaky with sleep, she finally got out of bed, put on a warm, silk-lined négligé, and stumbled to open the door.

Nick burst in through it like the north wind, as violent and as icy, clutching a newspaper in one hand. Gina looked at him wearily.

'Not tonight, Nick! I'm too tired.'

'Did Cameron stay that late?' he hissed, the glitter of his eyes frightening her and making her wake up fully.

'He drove me home...' she began, and he laughed harshly.

'How did I guess?'

'But he didn't come in!' she insisted, and his mouth curled in a cold smile.

'Not tonight? What about all the other nights?'

'There haven't been any other nights!'

Nick held out the newspaper, which was folded open at a large photograph of her and Mac. 'That isn't what it says here! How long have you been seeing him behind my back? Ever since the summer? Even though I'd asked you not to see him again? I could kill you!'

CHAPTER FOUR

'YOU, of all people, should know better than to believe what it says in a newspaper! Whatever they say is a tissue of lies!' Gina said, watching him nervously and wishing she hadn't opened the door.

'And the photo too—is that a tissue of lies?' grated Nick, the front door slamming behind him as he thrust the newspaper he held right under her nose. 'Look at it! Go on! Look at it!'

Gina couldn't help looking and what she saw made her bite her lip, her colour coming and going, her face crimson one second and white the next. She and Mac Cameron, closely entwined, his arm tightly round her waist, her hand curving close to his neck, her face turned up towards him, her eyes enormous, dreamy, in the flashlight . . . it was damning and she knew it as soon as she saw it. No wonder Nick had jumped to conclusions—anybody seeing that photograph was going to think the same thing!

She looked back at Nick reluctantly, and found him watching her with those darkened, hostile eyes. 'I'm sure Sir George taught you the old newspaper adage—one picture is worth ten thousand words!' he snarled. 'That one certainly is! It says it all, doesn't it?'

She swallowed. She had to make him believe that the photograph didn't mean what it seemed to mean, but she had a sinking feeling that he wouldn't listen. She had seen Nick in one of these black rages, and he was unreachable when he was like this. Unreachable—and unpredictable; she had no idea what he might do next.

'We were only dancing——!' she began huskily, and Nick interrupted.

'But intimately, Gina, very intimately!' His hard mouth twisted in a cynical sneer and she winced. It hurt to have him look at her with such contempt. 'After seeing this picture, it doesn't need much imagination to guess what was going to happen as soon as the two of you were alone!' he bit out.

'I told you, nothing happened! Mac didn't come up here! We aren't lovers. We never have been!' Her lips were trembling so much that it was surprising Nick heard a word she said.

He reached out suddenly and she gasped as his fingers dug into her shoulders. 'Stop lying! This picture has blown your cover, Gina!' he ground out. 'Do you take me for a fool? Don't lie to me again, or I swear I'll hit you! I'm here to force the truth out of you, and I want it all this time—the truth, the whole truth and nothing but the truth!

'I'm telling you the truth!' Gina was getting angry, herself, now, and she glared up at him, green eyes overbright with resentment. 'I can't convince you if you're determined not to believe me, but there's nothing going on between Mac and me!' she threw at him. 'And I'm not going to let you burst in here and push me around in the middle of the night. I'm tired and I need some sleep!'

'Do I have to tell you what I need?'

Nick's voice made her clench with a disturbing mixture of shock and excitement.

'Stop this, Nick!' she muttered, her mouth dry and every nerve in her body leaping.

'I haven't even started yet!'

'Then, don't, or... or...'

Her voice died away in a breathless stammer under those hard, grey eyes.

'Or what, Gina?' Nick icily mocked.

Gina couldn't get a sound out, her eyes on his dark face, still struggling to break away from him but without the strength to unlock his grip. He was far too strong, his fingers were like iron clamps on her warm, silk-clad flesh, and he knew it, watching her struggle and smiling with angry amusement at her helplessness.

'I've been playing a waiting game for a year now, and it hasn't got me anywhere at all, has it?' he said, and her nerves jangled wildly at something in his voice. 'Well, my patience has run out. When I saw that photo in the paper tonight it was like a kick in the guts. The thought of you with another man, lying to me about it, letting me think that there was nobody else in your life, that, however long it took, one day we would understand each other, and you'd come to me... and all the time you were secretly dating Cameron, behind my back! It drove me crazy to realise what a fool you'd made of me!'

'No, Nick, you're wrong, you've got it all wrong,' she protested, her heart pounding in her throat. Nick had been coming closer and closer for the last year, but she had managed to hold him at bay, like a lion-tamer controlling a wild animal with a combination of the lash and a calm, soothing voice. They were always together, in that cage—the office, or back here, in the apartment block, it was all the same, a circle with her and Nick in it, facing each other, locked in that mortal combat. But she had tried to face Nick out, keep her nerve, and only when she sensed he might attack had she been forced to hit out at him, to drive him back to a safe distance. So far it had always worked.

But now the wild animal was out of the cage and she had a disturbing feeling that he was out of control, too. He wasn't going to listen to anything she said, he was too angry.

But she tried again, driven by fear of what might happen next. 'I haven't been seeing Mac, I was amazed when I saw him in Sir Dermot's car——'

'Gaskell!' Nick bit out, scowling. 'He was there too, was he?'

'He invited me to the opening of this new club. Everyone who was there had been invited personally;

even the drinks were free until midnight, it seems. I don't
know how Sir Dermot got an invitation, but he's what
they call an angel, he backs all sorts of theatrical ven-
tures, so maybe he's one of Barry Eagle's backers? I
don't know. But he rang and asked me to be one of the
party he was taking, and I didn't like to refuse because
you'd made it clear you wanted to keep him on the board,
so I didn't want to offend him.' She paused, then burst
out with a sort of resentment, 'And, anyway, I like him,
I'm fond of him, I always will be, because he was——'

'The old man's godson! Do you think I ever forget
that?' snapped Nick. 'I might have known he'd come
into it. Sir George Tyrrell is always behind whatever
happens. He's been dead for a year, but he still domi-
nates everything you say and do and think, doesn't he?'

'Because he's dead doesn't mean I stop loving him!
Your father is dead, but everything he stood for is still
important in your life, isn't it?'

Nick's brows jerked together. 'Don't drag my father
into this! You have no idea how I felt about him.' Then
his mouth indented with wry cynicism and his face
changed slightly. 'Actually, neither have I,' he said in a
different tone, grimacing. 'I was never quite sure whether
I loved or hated my father; I hardly saw him when I was
a child, I was away at boarding-schools all the time, and
he left me with servants when I wasn't at school. Ours
was a very distant relationship during the early years. I
resented him because he'd taken me away from my
mother, yet he didn't take any interest in me once he'd
got custody.'

Gina remembered what his mother had told her, in
San Francisco, and her green eyes softened, but Nick
wasn't looking at her, he was staring over her head at
the wall, his face bleak. She knew he was remembering
his childhood and waited, hoping he would talk about
it, let her see inside his head, but he didn't. After a
moment he made an angry movement of the head, as if

shaking off those sad memories, and looked down at her again with impatience.

'Sir George wasn't your father, anyway—he was no blood relation of yours at all.'

'He took my father's place in my life, though, after my father died,' she said more gently. 'There was just the old man and me then, with James dead, too. Neither of us had anyone else, so it was natural for us to cling together—we needed each other.' She paused and gave him a quick glance, lowered her lashes to cloak her thoughts, then said softly, 'Why do you keep sniping at me about it? Why does it bother you so much that I loved Sir George?'

Dark colour ran up Nick's face; he looked at her, restlessly looked away. 'I'm jealous—is that what you're hinting at?' he muttered. 'Yes, all right, I'm jealous, damn you!'

'Of an old man? Who's dead anyway?' Gina said with husky incredulity.

'Of anyone who comes between us!'

Her heart turned over heavily and she could scarcely breathe. If only she could believe that his jealousy and anger meant that he loved her, but she knew that if she had slept with Nick a year ago he would have forgotten all about her by now.

'Don't start that again!' she muttered hoarsely. One thing she had learnt about him was that he was tenacious in getting what he wanted, would hang on like a bulldog, never let go, until he had finally succeeded, then he would move on without a backward glance, pursuing something else with the same fanatic determination. Gina didn't intend to be one of his past successes, devoured and then forgotten as Nick passed on to the next challenge.

'I never stopped!' Nick bit out, watching her in a way that made her nerves go crazy.

'I'm not even listening!' was all she said, though. Gina had learnt self-control the hard way, by having to do so.

Nick's mouth twisted angrily. 'As if I didn't know! That's the whole trouble. You won't listen!'

He knew her much better now than he had a year ago. She looked so gentle and feminine, yielding, sensual. But she could be as immovably determined as Nick, in her own way, which was why they were locked together in this no-win situation; neither of them ready to give in or walk away and neither of them getting what they wanted.

'I don't know how much more of this I can stand,' Nick said, changing his mood again and pleading, trying to get sympathy from her. Gina had loved him once and he knew it, constantly hoping to surprise that love in her again. But Gina would rather die than let him glimpse it.

She gave him a wry look, knowing what he was up to, and Nick scowled again.

'What have you got in your veins? Ice?'

She often wished she had. She had loved him deeply, once, and been badly hurt when she realised how treacherous he could be; betraying her, and the old man she loved like a father, to steal a business advantage. Nick had no scruples or conscience, and she couldn't forgive or forget what he had done.

But she couldn't entirely kill the feeling she had for him, either. She hated him and loved him all in the same breath, emotions twisting inside her like a snake, bitter and restless, poisoning her life.

'Just leave me alone, Nick, will you?' she said wearily.

'To have an affair with Mac Cameron?' His eyes flashed. 'Do you really think I would?'

'I am not having an affair with Mac! I just told you— Sir Dermot arranged the party last night, and I didn't know Mac would be there! But there he was, at the nightclub, sitting at my table—what was I to do? Ignore him? He asked me to dance, I couldn't refuse, could I? And that's when that picture was taken—I'll admit it looks as if we're…well, as if——' She broke off, flushed and stammering, and Nick's mouth twisted.

'As if the two of you are lovers! At least you admit that!'

She couldn't deny it, all she could do was protest, 'Whatever it looks like, it isn't true! He's a nice man and I like him, but he's in love with Molly Green, not me!'

Nick's eyes sharpened. 'What?'

Gina nodded. 'He told me all about it last night. I warned him I'd have to tell you, and he said go ahead, he can prove it and he will, in court, if he has to!'

Nick listened intently while she told him everything Mac had said. 'Did you believe him?' was all he said when she had finished, and Gina nodded.

'He was too upset to be lying! And, anyway, I don't think a man would lie about something like that, especially if he had to go public with it. As Mac said, it will probably wreck his career, because it destroys him as a sex symbol.'

Nick grimaced, shrugging. 'He has a point! In his shoes I certainly wouldn't want everyone to know. Most men's ego couldn't stand it. Masculinity is a touchy issue, a lot of it is all wrapped up in image, how other people see you—not just how women see you, either, but how other men view you, too. For an actor, of all people, image is everything.' He paused, his eyes wry. 'No, I agree, it's unlikely Cameron would make up a story like that!'

He walked away across her sitting-room and stood at the window, staring out across the moonlit river, and Gina watched him, wondering what he was thinking about.

There was a glistening sheen to his silvered black hair, where he had walked through the lightly falling snow. She could even see powdery snow on the wide shoulders of his expensive dark overcoat. He wore evening dress;

but he had taken off his black tie and undone the collar of his formal white shirt on his way home.

Gina remembered suddenly that he had been having dinner at Number Ten, Downing Street, that evening, along with a handful of other influential media people. That sort of social engagement was part of his role; he could be out somewhere every night of the week, if he chose, but Nick tried to keep those functions to a minimum. They made him impatient. He thought them a waste of time and was always eager to get back to work.

He must have picked up tomorrow's editions of all the papers on his way home. He often did call in at Barbary Wharf before heading back here for the night—maybe he had even been helping to get the paper to bed. Nick was a hands-on proprietor—he kept in touch with daily happenings on the newspaper even when he was abroad. It often infuriated people, especially the editor, Fabien Arnaud, who was always finding himself pushed aside while Nick took over and made the decisions.

'God in heaven,' said Nick harshly. 'What a mess. You realise what this means? That girl lied, and Valerie Knight was fool enough to buy it! We're going to have to pay Cameron huge damages. Well, that's her job gone! She can clear her desk tomorrow.'

'That's not fair!' Gina took a few steps towards him, her face indignant.

He swung round, his face furious. 'Fair? My God, she cost us a fortune and you want me to be fair to her?'

'You can't blame Valerie for everything. She believed in Molly Green, and so did I. We all did.' Gina gave him a pointed stare. 'I seem to remember you saying something about how lovely she was, and how it was obvious she wasn't the type to lie. It was true, too. There's something about her that makes everyone believe in her.'

Nick gave her a cynical smile. 'All women have it. Some more than others, but most of them can make a man believe up is down and black is white, just by opening their big, innocent eyes and giving him a sweet smile.'

She knew he was sniping at her, and looked away, out of the window, to stop herself losing her temper again. He had stopped accusing her, he was quieter, and she wanted to keep him that way.

Snow was still falling, blowing over the roof-tops, through the trees along the embankment. It looked as if winter was here to stay. There were icicles hanging from bare twigs, from iron railings, from the eaves of houses. The moon showed like a pale wraith through the clouds, heavy with snow yet to come, and there were no stars.

Gina felt oddly depressed suddenly. The city seemed empty, desolate; she shivered as she stared at it.

'No, it's not surprising that Cameron was taken in by Molly Green,' said Nick cynically, then broke off and began prowling up and down the room like a caged cat.

'What now?' asked Gina.

'I had a thought! Look, it's obvious that Cameron would rather settle out of court, which means he'll take less than he's asking for. We'll have to go carefully, it will be like walking a tightrope... if we offer too little, he could get angry enough to go ahead anyway. But I'll tell Guy to start negotiations at once.'

'But you won't fire Valerie Knight, will you?' she coaxed, smiling up at him.

Nick came closer, watching her intently. 'What will you give me if I don't?'

She stiffened like a poker, immediately alert to his change of mood. 'That's blackmail!'

His grey eyes taunted her. 'It doesn't seem excessive, one kiss in exchange for Valerie Knight's job!'

'How can you play games with people's lives like that?' she scornfully accused and saw dark red colour crawl up his face.

'You're a fine one to talk about playing games with people! Well, you've played with me once too often!'

He moved like lightning, his arm closing tightly around her waist. Gina gave a sharp cry of wordless protest, but he took no notice. He had her clamped remorselessly, and Nick never let go of anything he had seized.

Nick's face was very close, his eyes glittering, and sudden fever flared through her, burning and aching. She had fought against his desire many times, but it was hard to fight her own. She closed her eyes to shut out that dark face, but that was another mistake. It gave him an advantage he promptly took.

His mouth came down in compelling urgency; with a groan her mouth parted and Nick invaded it, the intimate probing of his tongue sending shudders of pleasure down her spine.

One kiss, she thought. That's all this has to be—one kiss, and I save Valerie Knight's job. Put like that it seemed rational—she could give herself permission to kiss him without guilt if she was only doing it to save Valerie's job.

Nick bent her backwards over his arm and she instinctively clutched at him, one hand in his thick, vibrant hair, the other gripping his shirt, to keep herself upright, while she yielded her mouth to him, her slender body seeming boneless in his hold.

That very masculine mouth was still moving against her lips: coaxing and seducing one minute, demanding and fierce the next, making her dizzy, her head spinning. She couldn't breathe, her head flung back, her russet hair tumbling like a fiery waterfall over her shoulders. She felt Nick's fingers in her hair, then his hand slid down, exploring the curves of her body.

She knew she had to stop this, that this was not 'just one kiss'; she had always known it was reckless and stupid to let him touch her, and he wouldn't stop if she didn't make him, but she felt so odd; her blood was singing in her ears and she was shaking violently. Nick slid her négligé off her shoulders, it fell to the floor and she stood there in her thin silk nightdress, Nick's hands burning through the fine material.

She heard him breathing thickly. He buried his face in her throat, kissing her skin hotly; and she began moaning, holding his head in her hands and trembling.

She wanted him so much that she was dying. Her knees were giving way. She could barely stand upright. Nick's mouth travelled down to the warm whiteness of her breasts and she gave a wild cry.

Afterwards, she couldn't quite remember whether she had fainted and fallen, or Nick had pulled her down, but somehow she ended up lying down, on the floor, with Nick half lying on her, kissing her with a passion which made her quiver in hungry response.

He hadn't said a word for a long time, and Gina was so dazed and confused by then that she wasn't able to think clearly. She felt him taking off his overcoat and jacket, but it didn't occur to her that he was shedding all his clothes. It only dawned on her what he had been doing when her hand slid down from his hair to his neck and then his shoulder, and met warm, bare flesh.

A gasp broke out of her and her eyes flew open in shock and dismay. Nick was almost naked by then, and Gina went scarlet, then white, before trying to scramble up, get away. Nick grabbed folds of her silky nightdress and pulled her back down to him.

'No, I can't, Nick...' she moaned, struggling.

'You want me as much as I want you!' he muttered, and she drew a shaky breath. She tried to deny it, but the lie stuck in her throat. She had wanted him for what seemed now an eternity; she had tried to shut off her desire, silence her heart, deny her body, but deep inside her the need and passion had grown until now. Nick's kiss had forced open the door and her feelings had escaped; she felt them fountaining out of her, wild with freedom.

Nick arched over her, holding her down by her shoulders, and Gina's green eyes widened and darkened as she looked up, seeing him naked for the first time. She couldn't stop staring, at the strong, wide shoulders, the deep chest, with its brown aureoles around the nipples, a wedge of black hair growing down to his flat stomach. He had the narrow waist and slim hips of an athlete, she thought, her eyes travelling down further.

She hadn't seen a man naked for years, and James had not matched Nick's physical power. Suddenly, she realised that she couldn't actually remember how it had felt to make love with James, or how he had looked, aroused, as Nick was now. Heat burned inside her, just looking at Nick's hard erection. If she had ever doubted that he really desired her, she had visible evidence of it now.

Nick was breathing thickly, watching her staring at him. 'Gina, my God, Gina...' he groaned hoarsely, and then he was kissing her again and she was lost in a whirlwind of wild sensuality which blew away every vestige of the past, all anger and resentment, all her doubts and fears. She had never in her life been so conscious of another body, or, come to that, the needs of her own. Nick's kiss made her pulse with sexual fever; she moved feverishly against him, touching him as intimately as he touched her, her hands discovering the physical reality of what her eyes had seen a moment ago: those shoulders, the wiry roughness of the dark hair on his chest, the smooth, flat planes of his stomach, the bony angle of his hips.

Only when he parted her thighs and slid between them did she feel a brief stab of fear, of uncertainty. She gripped his shoulders, holding him away, looking up at him shyly through flickering lashes.

'Nick,' she whispered with dry, shaking lips, 'Nick... wait...I'm afraid...' How could she explain that she felt like a virgin, that it was so long since James died that she couldn't remember how it had been, that she was nervous of this intimacy that might hurt?

'Don't be scared, Gina,' he said and smiled down at her as if he understood, even as if her fear pleased him. 'I won't hurt you, I'd never hurt you...relax...' And his hands softly stroked her inner thighs, caressing her there in a way that made her breath come fiercely, made the aching heat deep inside her worse.

Nick lowered his head to her breast, his mouth hot on her silky skin; she heard him murmuring passionately, but the words were lost, only the accents of tormented desire got through to her, and the clamour of her own hunger made her arch up to him, her arms around his body, pulling him into her.

As he entered her she felt not pain, nor fear, but an overwhelming sense of completion, as if she had always been unfinished, missing something without knowing what it was, and now Nick made her real and whole. She clung to him, holding him in her, possessing him; and their naked bodies became one, a fiercely driving energy building up as they moved against each other, in each other, pulsing and throbbing in waves of sensual pleasure.

The sexual tension inside her, in them both, tightened and increased with every movement until she was shuddering and crying out in intolerable need.

'Yes, Nick, yes...oh, Nick...' She caught her breath and then it escaped in a high, shuddering gasp. 'Nick!'

The spiral of tension broke and she fell as if from a great height; her eyes shut, her arms around him, moaning out her pleasure and the wild satisfaction he had given her, yet conscious all the time of Nick's long orgasm, his gasping breath, the deep groans he gave, as his body lay on her, shuddering ecstatically.

Afterwards, Gina lay as if dead, her arms splayed out on the carpet, her eyes shut and her breathing slowing from a ragged sound to a calmer note.

Nick lay on top of her for a moment or two while his body still vibrated, a slow trembling running through his muscles. His head had fallen against her naked breast, his breathing warm on her flesh, his lips softly mouthing one of her nipples.

As Gina came out of that almost deathlike trance, she grew conscious of Nick, of his weight pressing her down against the carpet, the intrusion of his body into hers, the possessive touch of his mouth on her breast, his hands idly wandering over her.

He touched her as if he owned her, she thought in sudden shock; then Nick raised his head lazily and smiled down at her, arrogant assurance in his face, and Gina felt her blood run cold.

For a year, ever since Sir George Tyrrell died, she had been controlling Nick in private and in public—saying no to him as a lover, and managing to block him at work if she did not agree with what he wanted to do on the *Sentinel*.

Tonight, though, the whole situation between them had changed. She had let Nick possess her, he had finally won their personal battle, and his grey eyes glittered with triumph, a renewed power. She sensed that things would never be the same again, either in private or at work.

Oh, how could I be so weak? she thought in desperation. What have I done?

CHAPTER FIVE

ONLY fourteen shopping days left till Christmas, Sophie thought as she walked from the underground station to Barbary Wharf at the end of that week. She had bought gifts for almost everyone, but so far she hadn't found anything for Uncle Theo. She would have to make time to trawl some of the antiquarian bookshops, or perhaps some specialist antique shops. It didn't have to be expensive, but she loved her uncle; she always tried to find him something unique, something he couldn't expect, and then watch his face light up as he unwrapped the surprise.

That was one of the most charming things about Uncle Theo—his childish delight in surprises. He had had so much tragedy in his early life, when terror struck his family and his country and he had to become homeless, a nomad, rootless and lonely; how had he retained the innocence and trust and sense of wonder of a child?

There was a lot more than that to Uncle Theo, of course! He was sophisticated, erudite, a man of the world, too, and a brilliant historian. It was a pleasure to work with him on his book. Sophie never regretted the bargain they had made, for she was as interested in his work as he was.

She wished he weren't quite so shrewd, though. Over the last few days, since the engagement party, she had several times caught him scrutinising her face, his eyes concerned. She hadn't confided in him, and did not intend to, but Uncle Theo knew her better than anybody in the world. She didn't have to tell him that something catastrophic had happened to her recently. He picked it up in the air whenever she was in the same room.

She frowned, wondering how to put him off the scent. Maybe she should drop some remark about not feeling very well lately? She was prone to pick up any germs that were wandering around, especially in winter, and he knew it.

This cold weather was enough to make anyone feel ill. It wasn't snowing today, but as she looked up at the grey sky, heavy with cloud, she shivered—it might yet snow later in the day, and she was glad she had put on her warmest coat.

She rounded the corner and could see Barbary Wharf—in winter it looked even more like a fortress, the high walls around it almost medieval, threatening, the dark glass in the windows sinister, secretive. But the central heating was very efficient, and would be full on today. She couldn't wait to get inside—she was dying for a cup of hot, strong coffee.

Others were streaming into the building, too: electricians headed for the print works, with its web offset and flexographic presses, its robots loading the giant paper reels which fed the press; telephonists from the advertising department who would sit at rows of desks all day with their headphones clamped over their heads, taking in advertising, large and small, over the phone; reporters and photographers, secretaries and porters, messengers and courier boys in warm, padded leather jackets and white helmets, huddled on their motorbikes, van drivers and packers from the despatch department.

Thousands of people worked in Barbary Wharf, although when the *Sentinel* was printed in Fleet Street there had been an even bigger workforce. Nick Caspian had sacked all the old printers when the paper moved down here. The ancient craft of printing born in the days of Caxton had been overtaken by complex electronic machinery, which only required supervision by electricians and machine minders.

As Sophie hurried through the Indy Road entrance she caught sight of a familiar figure on the walkway ahead of her.

Guy! She came to a stop, biting her lip. Ever since the night of the engagement party, when she ended up in bed with him, Sophie had felt that little jab of shock every time she saw him.

She had literally been saved by the bell—the telephone bell! But she still had not got over what had so nearly happened, and the very sight of him did something odd to her nerves.

In spite of the icy wind which whipped his dark hair about, and kept trying to wrench the wine-red scarf from around his neck, he was strolling along, obviously in no hurry to get to work. No doubt because he was too busy talking to the blonde girl walking beside him.

Sophie's teeth met as she recognised his companion. Valerie Knight! She slowed to keep a few steps behind them, watching them angrily.

Gib wouldn't like it if he could see Valerie smiling up at Guy like that. Sophie watched her fluttering her lashes in that phoney way and flirting like crazy. No, Gib would not like to see that at all. He had chased Valerie for a long time, and, having got her, he was openly possessive, especially where Guy was concerned. The two men bristled whenever they met—and Sophie was sure Valerie loved that; she was the type to enjoy being a *femme fatale*. She'd love it even more if they actually came to blows over her, no doubt.

Sophie scowled at the other girl's back. She didn't like her, she never had, and not just because she was jealous of her. Valerie was too brash, too streetwise; she had a hard, ambitious mind, which she cloaked behind that ultra-female exterior. She used her femininity ruthlessly to get what she wanted.

Men didn't seem to notice it, but other women did. Sophie did. She couldn't deny that Valerie was striking: she had a lovely face, a sexy figure. No, it was more than that—she looked like a film star, and she wore some outstanding clothes, too. Sophie stared at the outfit Valerie was wearing today—a full-skirted white fake fur coat trimmed at the collar and hem with black velvet bands; a matching white fake fur Russian-style hat, black leather gauntlets which stretched to her elbows and high-heeled, knee-high black leather cavalry boots.

Sophie wished she had the nerve to carry it off, but somehow she always ended up choosing classical clothes, quietly elegant, understated. That was her style, she knew the image she showed the world: tall, slender, with long, sleek legs and a calm, oval face, she always gave the impression of being self-sufficient and confident, and to some extent that was true. But there was an inner core of her nature which was not so sure of itself, or of life: which doubted and shrank back, was afraid.

That might have been why she spent a lot of time on her appearance, trying to build a glossy, confident shell: brushing her long, golden-brown hair into that chignon, choosing classy clothes which made her look immaculate and cool.

Really, she did not want to attract the sort of attention Valerie did. She preferred to keep men at a safe distance, and she succeeded.

That was why men didn't stare at her with their eyes on stalks the way they did at Valerie, who shrieked sex appeal and made men feel that she might just be available.

Sophie watched as Guy put an arm round Valerie, to steer her round a group of night workers leaving Barbary Wharf on their way home.

Sophie's mouth tightened. In spite of the fact that Valerie had just got engaged to someone else, obviously he couldn't take his eyes off her, let alone his hands!

He'd told her the other night that he was in love with Valerie, but Sophie couldn't understand it. Didn't he realise that he wasn't Valerie's type at all? Without ever discussing it with the other girl, Sophie was certain of that much. Valerie might automatically flirt with everything in trousers, but she wouldn't really be interested in a man like Guy. He was too clever, too serious-minded.

Not that it mattered to Sophie, of course! If he wanted to make a fool of himself, let him. But she had thought Guy had more sense.

Was he hoping Valerie would quarrel with Gib? That was on the cards, of course. The two of them were volatile, unpredictable, a little wild—that was what made them a natural pair, what drew them together. It could also tear them apart without warning.

But how could Guy have any self-respect if he hung around hoping to catch Valerie on the rebound? Sophie felt like hitting him. Where was his pride, for heaven's sake? She had been badly hurt by Gib, and she still ached inside whenever she thought of him, but her pride would never let her hang around, waiting for him to turn back to her. Once she knew it was over, she had lost any chance of getting Gib, she had made herself accept it. She'd die rather than let anyone, especially Gib, see she had been hurt.

As she followed the two of them across the foyer towards the lifts, she glanced casually through the glass doors into the Plaza, the open square in the centre of the complex, and with a little jab of surprise saw Gib. He had his back to her, he was walking into Torelli's snack bar, and on impulse she hurried over there, feeling faintly guilty and at the same time defiant. Well, why not?

If Valerie Knight could flirt with Guy, why shouldn't she talk to Gib? She might find out whether or not there was any trouble between him and Valerie.

As she came into Torelli's Gib looked round and gave her his familiar, light-hearted grin. 'Oh, hi, Sophie! Now, this is weird! A real coincidence! I was just telling Mrs Torelli you were part Italian, and saying what good pasta you cook.'

She flushed, laughing and shaking her head. 'Take no notice, it isn't that good!'

'Oh, yes, it is,' insisted Gib, his eyes dancing. 'Pity you're married, Roberto! Sophie is just the girl for you, she could take over all the cooking and do the accounts as well. She's not just a good cook, she's smart, too.'

'She couldn't do worse than his wife, that's for sure! Sandra can't cook pasta to save her life!' old Mrs Torelli snorted. She made no secret of the fact that she did not like her son's wife. Sandra Torelli had so far given her no grandchildren, a failure even more dire than her bad cooking.

'I didn't marry her for her pasta!' Roberto muttered, dark red in the face.

'Just as well! And, excuse me for asking, what did you marry her for? It's always been a mystery to me!'

'You've never liked Sandra!' Roberto growled, lapsing into Italian.

Sophie understood him perfectly; she was totally bilingual, since her father's mother had been an Italian and both English and Italian had been spoken in her home all her life, not to mention several other languages, including Hungarian. In fact, it had been languages, and their sense of being foreigners, that had brought her parents together. They had met at an international social club in London when they were in their early twenties.

Her mother had been the youngest in the Petofi family; she had been a child and had stayed behind with an older, married sister when Uncle Theo got out of Hungary in the aftermath of the Second World War. Then, when she was in her first year at university, the Hungarians rose against their Russian overlords.

The Russian tanks had ruthlessly crushed that revolt in November 1956, and thousands of Hungarians fled across the Austrian border. Mira Petofi had been one of them; she had brought nothing with her, arriving penniless in Vienna, but Uncle Theo had at once pulled every string he could to get her to England as a student. She got her degree, Uncle Theo found her work as a translator, and then she met Bruno Watson, fell in love and married him.

Mrs Torelli laughed angrily. 'Like her? What should I like? That she is a——'

'Mamma!' roared Roberto, incensed now.

Sophie and Gib exchanged wry looks. It was now a commonplace for the Torelli family to have one of their noisy squabbles while they were serving customers. People quite enjoyed the daily drama, the sense of living on the edge of Mount Etna in danger of imminent explosion, but it did make buying a cup of coffee a perilous event.

'What did you say you wanted, Gib?' asked Roberto, coldly turning his back on his mother.

'A cup of your coffee to take away, and a Danish!'

'I tell you... I knew she was no good the minute I saw her!' Mrs Torelli muttered in Italian. She dominated her two sons, who were scared stiff of her, loved her and resented her, all at the same time, but she had a soft spot for Gilbey Collingwood, whose charm and teasing smile had won her over at first sight. 'But you made your bed, you must lie on it,' she told Roberto, then pushed him aside and beamed at Gib.

'I knew you'd be in for it, so I kept you the best Danish we got today—a double custard with apricots, your favourite! You want it hot? I'll put it in the microwave, only take half a minute.'

'If I hadn't just got engaged to someone else, I'd ask you to marry me,' said Gib, and she laughed loudly, shaking her head at him.

'You wicked boy! I could be your grandma.'

'You're much too beautiful to be my grandma—she's got a moustache!'

'Now, don't you be rude about your grandma. She loves you, I bet she loves you. Who wouldn't love a boy like you, with a heart of gold and that lovely smile? Some mothers have all the luck. Me, I got this idiot, here, who goes and marries a no-good from God knows where!'

'What can I get you, Sophie?' Roberto asked in Italian, and she smiled back, shaking her head.

'Nothing, at the moment, but could you make me some salad sandwiches for lunch and a box of fruit salad, in natural juice, and I'll pick them up at around one?'

Roberto noted the order down, nodding. 'Sure, OK.'

The microwave beeped, and Mrs Torelli got out the hot Danish pastry, using plastic tongs, slid it into a bag, along with the coffee in a waxed cup with a lid on it. Gib paid. *'Arrivederci!'* they said to the Torellis, who chorused, *'Ciao!'* for once in unison.

As they left the snack bar a few flakes of snow came drifting down. Gib paused, looking up at the sky, grimacing.

'Here we go again!' He put an arm round her and ran with her back into the foyer where the central heating hit them with a wave of welcoming hot air.

Gib followed her into the lift, and smiled down at her. 'I didn't really get a chance to talk to you at our party, did I? Thanks for the present; Valerie and I loved it.'

She wondered if he even remembered what she had chosen for them—a rather beautiful sea-green glass salad bowl with matching servers, made by one of the best English glass makers.

'I'm glad you approved,' she rather drily said.

'Did you enjoy the party?' Gib asked quickly, not quite meeting her eyes. 'When I looked round for you, to have a word, you'd vanished.'

'I drank too much,' she lied. 'Guy took me home.'

Gib made a wry face. 'Did he now? Well, I don't blame him—you looked lovely, you always do.'

She looked down, guessing that he didn't recall what she had worn or how she had looked. She had watched him and she knew he had had eyes only for Valerie.

But she pretended to smile. 'Thanks.' Melancholy flooded through her as the lift stopped and Gib walked out on his own floor. Every time she said goodbye to him it felt as if it was forever, now, and in a way it was— she had to start meaning it.

She found Guy in her office, standing by her desk, leafing through the pile of mail which was sitting in her in-tray.

He looked up, his eyes sharp and cold. 'You're late!' Ever since the other night there had been an atmosphere between them, and she avoided looking at him, a flush crawling up her cheeks.

'Sorry,' she said brusquely, taking off her smooth-fitting olive-green coat and hanging it up. 'I got held up.'

'By the weather?' Guy glanced out of the window. 'I see it's snowing again. We may have a hard winter ahead—still, a white Christmas could be fun. I shall spend mine in the country, with my family, I suppose. Will you have a family Christmas, Sophie?'

'Unless I want to be torn limb from limb—yes.' She was so nervous that she chattered as she put on the coffee machine, then sat down behind her desk, unlocked her desk drawers and began the usual routine of the day.

'They expect me to be there,' she said. 'They like to gather everyone back into the fold at Christmas. Both sides of the family have the exile mentality; they feel they're somehow missing the real Christmas by not being somewhere else—every year nostalgia comes welling up in them and they talk about the past all the time, about Hungary or Italy, or their childhoods.'

'The uncle whose house you live in is Hungarian, isn't he? How long has he been here?' Guy asked, perching on the edge of her desk and making her intensely conscious of him in a way she never had been before. But then until a few days ago she had been unaware of what lay beneath the expensively tailored suits he wore. It was hard to forget it, having seen him naked. To her dismay she kept getting flashing images of him that night; even though she kept her gaze fixed elsewhere.

To cover her confusion, she kept on talking, which was unusual for her. Sophie had always been reluctant to talk about her private life, her family or her background.

Guy listened with intent interest as she told him, 'Uncle Theo has lived in London, in the same house, for over forty years, but he still thinks like a refugee, and my mother is just as bad.'

'She's Hungarian, too?'

Sophie nodded. 'She's his sister, but she hasn't been here as long as he has, only since 1956.'

Guy's eyes narrowed thoughtfully. 'Ah, the Hungarian revolution? I read a book about that recently. I forget the author's name, but I'll lend it to you if you'd like to read it.'

'We probably have it. Uncle Theo buys every book on Hungary that gets published!' she said wryly and laughed.

Guy shifted closer, leaning down to look into her amber eyes; and she heard the blood beating in her ear, as if she had suddenly developed hypertension. How long was it going to take her to forget the events of that night after the engagement party? she wondered desperately, aware of the colour coming and going in her face.

To her relief, the telephone rang just at that second, and Sophie answered it while Guy watched her, a glimmer of mockery in his eyes.

'It's Mac Cameron's solicitor—do you want to take the call in your office?' she murmured, not looking at him.

He shook his head and took the receiver from her. 'Get me a cup of that coffee before it gets cold,' he told her.

She reluctantly obeyed, hearing him talking behind her as she poured the coffee. 'Yes, Guy Faulkner here. Good morning, Artie—how are you? Yes, I'm fine too.' Then he fell silent, listening, his foot tapping in a rhythm which was familiar to her by now and meant that Guy was concentrating hard, and very interested. 'Well, I'm very glad to hear it,' he said. 'As soon as you hear the results, let us know, will you? Thanks for the call. Keep in touch.'

He hung up and Sophie gave him a questioning look. Guy smiled at her, satisfaction in his face.

'Cameron has agreed to have a fresh series of tests to check whether or not he can have a child, and of course one of them will be the DNA test, so with any luck we should resolve the case quite soon now.'

Sophie's face lit up. 'That's wonderful! Not just for the paper. I know it will get the *Sentinel* off the hook, but I was thinking about the baby, and Molly Green. If the tests prove the baby is his, think what it will mean for them!'

Guy regarded her drily. 'Don't be too optimistic, Sophie. Leopards don't change their spots very easily, and even if Mac Cameron drops the case against the *Sentinel* he may still not admit to being the father. After all, that would mean paying Molly a lot of money!'

'That's a rather cynical way of looking at it!'

'Just realistic,' he said. 'We'd better do the letters now.' Picking up his coffee, he walked through into his own office and she followed him with her own coffee, the letters which seemed to need an immediate reply, and her notepad.

They just had time to finish the dictation before Guy had to go up to a meeting with Sean Yates, the managing director of the paper, Fabien Arnaud, the editor, and some other senior editorial executives. They were having a policy discussion, re-evaluating the change in direction which Nick Caspian had set afoot in the *Sentinel* when he took over. There had been various problems, not least a rash of threats of legal action from people who felt they had been unfairly treated in the newspaper's columns.

'Nick left for Luxembourg suddenly last night, a problem he had to deal with in person,' Sean Yates told them all as he opened the discussion in the boardroom. 'He sends his apologies and asked me to stand in for him. We have another apology for absence.' He smiled round the table at them all. 'Jack Horton's wife rang to say he has a hacking cough...you know how weak his chest is lately. I wouldn't be surprised if Jack decided to take early retirement soon. Anyway, he's staying in bed.'

'On a day like this it is probably the best place to be!' Guy murmured, and the men all looked out of the window at the livid skies.

'There's more snow on the way, they said on breakfast TV,' said someone and there were groans around the table.

'Well, thank the lord I'm going to Florida for Christmas,' Sean said.

There was general laughter. 'You're not going there for the sunshine, Sean, you're going there for the golf! Doesn't your wife mind going away at Christmas?'

'She spends Christmas watching TV anyway, so it doesn't matter to her where she is!' He looked at the clock on the wall. 'Shall we get started?'

Guy walked back into the office and found Sophie eating her lunch at her desk.

She looked round at him, flushing. 'Oh...sorry...did you want something?'

'No, don't let me interrupt your meal.'

'I've more or less finished!'

'Is there any coffee?'

'Yes, it's still hot. Shall I bring a cup to your office?'

'I'll get it myself,' Guy said, walking over to the coffee-pot, and poured himself a cup of black coffee with which he sat down on the edge of her desk, as he had earlier that day. Sophie neatly disposed of the remains of her lunch, wrapped in the waxed paper in which it had come, and put it into the waste paper basket.

'I've got all the letters ready for you to sign,' she said, getting up.

'No hurry. It's still lunchtime. Sit down again.' He gave her a glance through his lashes, sipping his coffee. 'I was just thinking about your mother. How old was she when she left Hungary?'

Sophie uneasily sat. They had worked with each for months now without learning very much about each other, and that was how she liked it. She was wary of close relationships and she was especially wary of Guy Faulkner after the other night. She did not want him to know too much about her.

'She was seventeen,' she said shortly.

'How did she get out of the country?'

'Walked.'

'Is it a state secret?' he mocked, his mouth crooked. 'Why are you so secretive?'

'I don't know why you want to know...'

His black lashes lifted and his blue eyes shone ironically at her.

Rather sulkily, Sophie said, 'She walked there, through woods and fields, over the Austrian border, mostly travelling by night, to avoid being seen.'

'Was she alone?' he asked and Sophie nodded.

'My grandparents had been dead for years, and the rest of the family didn't want to leave. My mother knew the border area because we had relatives there; she worked out a route and set off alone.'

'I'm impressed,' he said, and for a second she thought he was making fun of her, but then she saw that his face was serious. 'How did she get to England?'

'Uncle Theo arranged that. He has friends all over the place, he made phone calls, talked to people, and got her over here. She lived with him, of course; there's lots of space.'

'But she doesn't live there now?'

'No, of course not. She lives with my father, in Dulwich.'

'But you prefer to live with your Uncle Theo?'

'It's an easier journey to work every day, and I have more independence.'

'Uncle Theo works at the BBC, I remember you once said?'

'Part-time. He's a historian, he's writing a history of Hungary at the moment. I type it for him, and try to help him with his English. It's pretty good, but he does miss out on nuances from time to time.'

'Has he ever written anything else? Anything that has been published?'

She bristled. 'Yes, a history of 1848.'

'The year of revolution in Europe! Yes, of course, a lot was going on in Hungary, too, at the time. Kossuth, wasn't it? Is it still in print? I'd like to buy it.'

'I can lend you a copy, if you really want to read it,' Sophie said uncertainly.

'I do, thanks; I'll remind you about that,' he said, finishing his coffee and putting down the cup. 'What did you mean about your mother and uncle thinking like refugees?'

She flushed. 'Did I say that? Well, it's true—they've never felt at home here, they think of themselves as Hungarians, all their friends are Hungarian, they read Hungarian newspapers, even eat Hungarian food a lot of the time.'

'Well, they were both of them more or less adults when they left, weren't they? It's only natural. Have you ever been to Hungary?'

She shook her head. 'But I feel as if I have because I hear so much about it, especially at Christmas. We don't have turkey and Christmas pudding, we have goose, served with a spicy sauce, made from an old Magyar recipe handed down in my family for generations. Sweet peppers, paprika, tomatoes and caraway seeds ... I expect you'd hate it.'

'It sound delicious!'

She gave him a startled look, not having expected that. She would have thought Guy's culinary tastes were likely to be very conventional, very English. He grinned at her teasingly.

'And what do you have for pudding?'

'Plum dumplings Mamma makes, they're very rich, too, and served with cream sprinkled with cinnamon.'

'Even more delicious,' he said. 'Tell me some more...'

She laughed. 'Well, Uncle Theo chooses the wines. He found a Hungarian wine merchant somewhere in London—with the goose, we usually have Egri Bikavér, they call it Bull's Blood in English, and, with the pudding, Tokaji Aszu, a dessert wine which is very sweet. My father hates it! He doesn't like sweet wines.'

'Your father can't be Hungarian, though—not with a surname like Watson!'

'Good heavens, no!' Sophie laughed at the very idea. 'But he's of Italian descent, and he has the exile mentality, too, he doesn't feel really English. That's what brought him and Mamma together—they both felt out of place.'

'It has to be his mother who was Italian...' Guy worked out.

'Yes, she was from the Italian lake region, near Lake Lugano, a tiny medieval town called Campione d'Italia. She first came to England to work as a cook for a rich Italian family in the diplomatic service, way back in 1910. She was engaged to someone back home, they were going to get married when her father paid her dowry. In those days, they still insisted on that, and she was saving all her wages for her trousseau. Then in 1912 she met my grandfather one day in Hyde Park, and three weeks later eloped with with him.'

'What a fantastic story!' Guy looked amused; she could see he wasn't sure if he believed her.

'Well, it's true, every syllable of it!' she said huffily. She had heard these family anecdotes all her life, but she knew that other people were incredulous if she ever told them about her family. That was why she preferred not to talk about them. She didn't know what had possessed her to talk about them to Guy Faulkner, of all people!

He gave her a shrewd glance. 'I'm sure it is.'

Rather stiffly, she said, 'Her employers would never have let her marry my grandfather. They knew about her fiancé back home. They'd promised her parents that they would take care of her while she worked for them, that she would be safe with them. She only had one afternoon off a week, and then she was only allowed out if she was with one of the older servants. Her employers didn't realise this other woman had a boyfriend, too, and left my grandmother to her own devices. But she would have been packed off back to Italy if the family she worked for had even suspected she had met a man. They certainly wouldn't have approved of my grandfather.'

'Why not?' Guy asked curiously. 'Wasn't he respectable?'

'He was poor,' she bluntly said. 'He was a professional musician. He played the organ in his village church on Sundays, and at weddings, and played the fiddle at dances. He earned enough to live on but he would never be rich. She knew her family wouldn't think it was a good match. So she and my grandfather ran off to Scotland and got married over the anvil at Gretna Green.'

Guy laughed loudly. 'You certainly have a dramatic family! Then what happened?'

'They lived happily ever after,' Sophie said rather tartly.

'Of course,' he murmured, his smile ironic.

She insisted, frowning, 'Their marriage was completely happy, they had a wonderful life together and they died within a week of each other.'

'What about her family in Italy? Did they forgive her?'

'Not until her first son was born—my father. She called him Bruno, which was her father's name. But she never got back to Campione d'Italia while her parents were alive, which was sad.'

'It sounds to me as if she was only too happy to stay away,' Guy said cynically. 'After all, she could have stayed there and got married, but she didn't. She came to England and married your father in a great hurry.' He gave her a sideways glance, his mouth twisting. 'But then women always do precisely what they want to do, and afterwards blame it all on someone else! Usually, on a man!'

'Is that a dig at me?' Sophie flared, her colour high.

'Why, do you recognise the description?' he drawled.

'No, I don't! But I noticed the pointed way you looked at me as you said it!'

'I was remembering how you got me into bed the other night . . .'

'I did *what*?' She turned scarlet.

'And then next morning slapped me down for having accepted the invitation!' he finished coolly.

'I didn't offer any invitation! I was feeling depressed, and you took advantage by trying to seduce me!'

'Trying?' he repeated, and laughed mockingly. 'I didn't just try, I managed it. If that phone hadn't rung——'

'I'd have thrown you out of my flat!' she angrily interrupted.

'You didn't even want me to answer the phone,' he reminded her.

'You know very well why that was! I didn't want anyone to know you were there!'

He ignored that. His voice mocking, he said, 'But I had to leave, and you had time to think, didn't you?' He suddenly leaned forward to take hold of her chair with both hands, imprisoning her.

Startled, Sophie looked up and found him much too close; those cool blue eyes probing her expression.

'Gilbey Collingwood was never the right man for you, anyway. Forget him, Sophie!'

'The way you're forgetting Valerie Knight?' she scornfully demanded.

He looked at her in blank bewilderment. 'What's that supposed to mean?'

'I saw you with her this morning. I saw you smiling at her, putting your arm round her—you won't forget her that way!'

A teasing brightness came into his eyes. 'You sound jealous, Sophie!'

Her nerves skidded and she looked away, her face burning. Jealous? For a second she thought about it, appalled, then she pulled herself together. She must not let him think for an instant that he had hit any sort of target! She couldn't be jealous, of course. It wasn't possible. But the mere suggestion had disturbed her.

'Jealous, over you?' she threw back at him, and laughed coldly. 'Don't kid yourself!'

'Then why are you so angry?' he asked in a soft voice, and the question echoed in her head.

Yes, why was she so angry at the idea of him and Valerie Knight? She couldn't deny that when she'd seen them this morning she had wanted to hit him, but she tried to keep that admission out of her face.

'I just don't like getting advice from someone who can't manage his own life, let alone run mine!' she snapped.

He came even closer, invading her body space, his face inches away from her own.

'Is that all it is? Sure about that?'

She wasn't, but she needed time alone to think about the implications of what she was feeling, and she certainly wasn't going to let Guy Faulkner glimpse her uncertainty. He was too quick to take advantage of any weakness he noticed. No wonder he was such a clever lawyer; he would be lethal in a courtroom, and she wondered why he had never become a barrister, and that reminded her of the man she had met at the nightclub. No doubt Andreas Kirk was pretty lethal, too.

'Certain,' she said flatly, and then, before he could say anything else, she asked in a casual voice, 'By the way, have you ever heard of a barrister called Andreas Kirk?'

Guy straightened, his blue eyes narrow and alert. 'What about him?'

'I met him the other night, that's all, and I was curious about him.'

'Were you?' Guy said drily. 'Well, it isn't wise to be too curious about Andreas Kirk; he has some very dangerous acquaintances. He specialises in criminal law and some of his clients are not men you'd like to meet on a dark night.'

'Yes, Tom said something like that.'

Guy's stare sharpened. 'So, it was Tom who introduced you to Andreas Kirk? That's the trouble with crime reporters, they mix with very shady characters. I warned you Tom wasn't your type, didn't I?'

'You don't know what my type is!' she said crossly, and he gave her a mocking smile.

'Don't be too sure about that. I'm finding out a lot about you.'

Sophie stiffened. Was that why he had asked her all those questions? Or was he talking about something very different? Her skin grew hot at the memory of that night, in her flat, and she lowered her lashes to hide her reaction from him. Yes, he had found out a lot about her that night and she wished to God he hadn't!

Coolly, Guy murmured, 'I've often wondered what was behind that calm mask you wear around the office. You seem very much in control, always efficient, capable, a little remote—and that's deliberate, isn't it? You've gone to a lot of trouble to keep the real Sophie hidden away.'

She pretended to laugh, but the sound quivered slightly. 'The real Sophie? Who's she?'

She had meant to be funny, but the question came out shakily, as if she didn't know the answer. She could have kicked herself!

'I'm not entirely sure yet,' he murmured. 'But the other night I got past the mask, and found a very passionate woman behind it.'

'Oh, shut up!' He was getting far too close, in every sense of the word, and she found it disorientating.

His hands pinned her shoulders back against the chair while he watched her, his blue eyes merciless.

'What's the matter, Sophie? What are you afraid of? I don't need to be a psychoanalyst to realise that your passion for order, for being conventional, not standing out in a crowd, comes from living in a family who are always aware of being outsiders and exiles.'

'I love my family!' she angrily defended.

He smiled at her, a sort of tenderness in his face for a second.

'I'm sure you do, but, all the same, you've been reacting against them all your life, trying to find your own values, your own place in the world.'

Uneasily, she shrugged. 'I suppose we all do that.'

'Of course we do. It's part of growing up, separating from our parents, learning to be ourselves. And it explains a lot about you, including why you were attracted to someone like Gilbey Collingwood. He's a very popular guy—everywhere he goes he fits in, and he has no hang-ups, no angst to contend with! When you were with him you felt you belonged, too, didn't you?'

'Will you stop trying to psychoanalyse me?' Sophie said irritably, pushing him away so that she could get up. She struggled out of the chair but tripped over her own feet and sprawled heavily forward. Guy caught her in his arms. For one second she lay there, helpless, then his head came down, and panic raced through her.

His mouth fastened on hers before she could pull back, and as it touched her she felt a wild rush of sensation. It had the strangest effect on her.

The room started going round and round; she was dizzy, she couldn't keep her eyes open any more. She clutched at him, trembling, deaf and blind to everything else for that moment, aware only of his mouth moving urgently on her own, of a hot ache deep inside her body.

Time seemed to stop, and then it began again. Guy lifted his head, his breathing audible; her eyes opened with slow reluctance, and they looked at each other.

Then Guy smiled and she read triumph in that smile and felt rage rush through her like a forest fire through dry brushwood.

Breaking away from him, she furiously stammered, 'You...you promised...when I said I was leaving, you promised...it had been a mistake, it would never happen again, if I stayed, you said! I can't go on working for you if you're going to grab me every time we're alone!'

'I didn't grab you, you grabbed me! You threw yourself at me!'

'I tripped!' she fiercely protested. 'That didn't give you *carte blanche* to kiss me!'

Eyes wide and innocent, he said, 'But I thought that was what you wanted!'

'You thought nothing of the kind, you liar!'

His smile mocking, he said, 'What else was I to think? And you can't deny you kissed me back!'

She couldn't deny it. She wished she could, glaring at him.

'Of course,' Guy softly assured her, 'if you don't want me to kiss you, I won't, but stop confusing me by throwing yourself at me like that.'

Sophie was so angry that she picked up her coffee-cup and hurled it across the room at him. It missed Guy, but hit the wall just behind him and smashed into dozens of sharp fragments with a sound like an explosion.

She was horrified by her own violence, and stood there, her hands clenched at her sides, breathing raggedly.

'Well, well, well,' murmured Guy, his brows lifting. 'You get more interesting every day!'

She was still absorbing that mocking comment when the phone rang, making them both start. It was Guy who got to it first; Sophie was too off balance.

'Legal department,' he said brusquely, and then his brows met as he listened. He slowly turned his head to stare at Sophie, his thin, hard face enigmatic.

Sophie was still coping with the after-effects of her outburst of temper; she wasn't really thinking about the phone call, which was probably for Guy, anyway. It was shocking to her that she should have lost control like that—she couldn't ever remember feeling that angry, or, at least expressing her anger so openly. She had spent her life hiding what she felt behind a calm, bland mask. What on earth was happening to her?

Guy held out the phone. 'For you,' he said, in a dry, flat voice. 'Andreas Kirk.'

CHAPTER SIX

SOPHIE hesitated before she walked over to take the phone, evading Guy's eyes, and turned away from him before she started speaking.

'Hello? This is Sophie Watson.'

The deep, resonant voice was instantly familiar, although they had only met that once. 'Hello, Sophie—this is Andreas Kirk, we met at the Blue Penguin the other night, remember?'

'Yes, of course,' she said huskily, intensely conscious of Guy right behind her, listening to every word.

There was a smile in Andreas Kirk's voice, as though her huskiness amused him. No doubt he was placing a very different construction on it, but there was nothing Sophie could do about that.

'I hope it is OK for me to ring you at work. I didn't have your home number, of course,' he murmured.

'Well, I am very busy...'

'Then I'll be quick! I won't beat around the bush, either—Sophie, I'd like to see you again; could we have dinner?'

'Oh...' Sophie let out a faint gasp of surprise, completely at a loss. 'Well, I...'

She didn't know what to say, torn between an intrigued curiosity about him, and her usual wary caution where men were concerned, especially men like him. Guy hadn't needed to warn her that Andreas Kirk had 'dangerous acquaintances'. Even if Tom hadn't told her first, Sophie's own instincts would have sent up an alarm the minute she set eyes on him.

'I think we might have a lot in common,' Andreas Kirk coaxed, but she frowned, not at all sure they would.

Tom moved on the edge of the criminal world, too, because his job demanded it, but there was an open cheerfulness about Tom that protected him from the corruption he encountered. Andreas Kirk was very different. She sensed a shadow behind him, a darkness at his centre, and she didn't want to get involved with him.

'Look, Mr Kirk——' she began, and he interrupted softly.

'Won't you call me Andreas? I've been using your first name!'

She hesitated, her flush deepening. 'Andreas, then...thank you for asking me...'

At that moment, Guy shifted position, moving round the desk so that he could see her face. Startled, Sophie found herself looking into his blue eyes. He frowned at her, shaking his head.

'Tell him no!'

She stiffened in resentment. Who did he think he was? And what made him think he could dictate to her like that? Her private life was no concern of his. Maybe he imagined that what had happened between them the other night made her his property, gave him some sort of proprictorial rights over her? Well, if that was what he thought he had a shock coming!

Andreas said in her ear, 'What about tonight, for instance?'

She almost said she wasn't free, but she wanted to defy Guy openly, to make him see he couldn't order her around. 'Tonight?' she said. On Fridays she usually went to evening school, but there wouldn't be any class meetings during the Christmas period, so tonight she would be free.

Defiantly, she outstared Guy's angry eyes.

'Yes, I'd love to have dinner tonight, Andreas,' she said.

Guy's face tightened, he turned on his heel and walked out of the room without a word. Sophie felt her own tension flow out with him. Deflating, she sat down behind her desk.

'That's wonderful, Sophie—now, can I pick you up? Where do you live?'

She absently told him, staring at Guy's closed door.

'I'll be there at seven-thirty. Until then...'

Andreas Kirk rang off with a click and Sophie slowly replaced her own phone, her hand still shaking.

What had possessed her to agree to meet the man? She hadn't wanted to see him again! But she knew perfectly well why she had done it. Out of a contrary desire to do whatever Guy did not want her to do—and that was crazy and flew in the face of her own common sense! She didn't understand herself any more.

Until the last few days she had had a calm, perfectly friendly, if businesslike, relationship with Guy. They had worked well together, she had always respected and admired him, not least because of the determined way he had switched his career from journalism to the law and then made himself into an expert on the law as it related to journalism.

She could remember saying to some of the other girls who worked in Barbary Wharf, 'It's exciting working for a boss like him! It makes you think...well, if he can do it, why shouldn't I?'

'Thinking of becoming a lawyer, Sophie?' Roz Amery had asked her, lifting her eyebrows in the superior way she had at times, and some of the other girls had giggled.

Sophie remembered being furious. She had glared back at Roz, bristling. 'I haven't made up my mind what I want to do, yet; but I'm sure about one thing—nothing's impossible if you're determined enough. That's what Guy has proved to me.'

And Roz had stared at her for a minute, then suddenly smiled with enormous warmth and approval. 'Good for you! I couldn't agree more.'

Relaxing a little, Sophie had said, 'I think I'll take some evening classes this autumn, then one day I can move on to some career a good deal more interesting than just being someone's secretary.'

'You have a head start since you already speak several languages fluently; that will come in handy with a number of jobs!' Roz had pointed out.

Sophie had given her a shy look. 'Do you think I might ever be able to switch to reporting? Foreign reporting?'

Roz had laughed abruptly, then she had said in a wry voice, 'Well, you have the right background for it. As you just said, nothing is impossible!'

That had been enough encouragement for Sophie, who had started a series of evening classes studying various aspects of journalism. Once, she had casually mentioned to Guy what she was doing. He had shot her a narrow-eyed stare, and had not appeared to be too pleased by the news.

'Does that mean I shall be losing you one of these days?'

'Eventually, yes, I hope so. If I can get a job on the editorial side of the *Sentinel*, or some other paper.'

Guy had frowned. 'I didn't know you wanted to be a reporter. What put the idea into your head?'

'You did!'

'I did? I can't remember saying anything that might have given you any such idea!'

'You showed me that anyone can do anything,' Sophie had told him quietly. 'You did, after all.'

That had made him flush a little, surprise in his blue eyes, then he had smiled at her. 'I'm flattered, Sophie. But you do realise, as you're working every day and only attending evening classes, it will take a few years before you are qualified to get a job as a reporter?'

She had lifted her chin. 'I know. I've thought it all out, the way you must have done. You must have made up a game plan for your life, it must have taken years to study law—but you had the tenacity to stick to it and finish your degree. I'm prepared to wait and work for what I want, too.'

He had nodded, his mouth crooked, saying, 'Well, good luck!' and she had felt a warmth between them, an understanding they hadn't had before. After that day they had worked together even more smoothly, until the other night, until what happened after Gib's engagement party.

All the tension which continually churned around inside her sprang from that night, and, far from getting better as time went on, it seemed to be getting worse.

Wrenched by a sigh, she stared out of the window at the whirling snow. If she had been her usual sensible self, she would never have agreed to have dinner with a man like Andreas Kirk.

Gina Tyrrell was staring out at the snow, too, blindly, without seeing the whirl of flakes blowing past, the delicate crystals forming on the windows like frosted lace. Her green eyes were haunted by regret and angry self-accusation. She had hardly slept for days, her mind obsessed with Nick, with images of them in bed, with the incredible intensity of what he had made her feel, with a hunger she still felt, but, at the same time, with shame and guilt because she hated herself for giving in to him and her own terrible need—and most of all with fear of what might come next.

She knew Nick Caspian too well now to believe he would be satisfied with one night of love. He would be back, and Gina was no longer quite so sure she would be able to reject him. Oh, she might deny his passion—but how was she going to deny his tenderness?

He had carried her into her bedroom after they made love, that night; had got into bed with her and held her cradled on his body, kissing her hair, touching her with a gentle tenderness that she couldn't get out of her mind.

'You're so lovely. Your body makes me go dizzy. I'd like nothing better right now than to make love to you again, but I'm too shattered by the first time,' he murmured in sleepy self-derision. 'You just used up all my energy, woman!' He yawned, not seeming to notice her frozen silence. 'But it was worth it...' Another yawn and then silence, and after a moment she realised that he was asleep.

She cautiously shifted sideways, intending to escape, but in his sleep he had turned heavily and his arm had fallen across her, like an iron bar, trapping her. She lay still, for a while, then tried again, wriggling softly in the hope of sliding out from under the arm. But although he didn't wake up he tightened his grasp of her, moving closer until his back was pressing against hers, and after that Gina gave up trying to get away.

She lay awake all night, in torment, listening to his breathing, right behind her ear; feeling the warmth radiating from the naked body lying so close that they were almost one, lungs drawing air in and out at the same time, their hearts beating with the same strong rhythm.

When Nick did wake up and stirred, yawning, she knew when he became aware of her, when he remembered the night before, his whole body stiffening, his arms tightening again, his warm flesh moving in a way that sent an erotic shudder through her.

She didn't give a sign, though, her eyes shut tight, while she tried to breathe as if she were sound asleep.

The next few moments were pure torture for her. Nick began to play with her, caress her, with hands and mouth—butterfly kisses which fluttered from her bare shoulders down her smooth-skinned back to her buttocks and the backs of her legs, while his hands explored the front of her body; the white fullness of her breasts, the small, hard nipples, the slim waist, the rounded curve of her hips, the deep indentations where her thighs began. Fire burnt along her nerve paths, made her painfully, intensely, wildly, aware of her own body and of his, made her ache with a bitter desire to turn into his arms and kiss him, touch him, with the same desire with which he was touching her.

But she fought down those impulses; lay stiff and unresponsive although she was in the worst torment of her life.

At last, Nick sighed and lay still, and she sensed that he had given up trying to arouse her. He slid out of the bed, softly trod out of the room. She heard him go into the bathroom, heard the shower running, heard him towelling himself. Then Nick came into the bedroom again and she kept as still and silent as a trapped animal pretending to be dead.

He stood in the doorway, watching her, listening to her breathing.

'I'm going now, Gina,' he said levelly. 'You can stop pretending to be asleep. It won't do you any good, anyway. I learnt too much last night—you won't be able to look me in the eye and tell me you don't want me, not any more.'

She bit down on her inner lip and tasted the salt of her own blood, but she managed not to cry out.

Nick laughed shortly. 'I'll see you at work,' he said, and then he left.

She listened to every movement he made, heard him walking through her apartment, heard him gathering up his clothes, heard him walk out of the front door and close it quietly behind him.

As soon as the door was shut Gina burst into terrible weeping, her face buried in her pillow, her body shuddering and trembling, icy cold.

It was a long time before she felt able to get up. She went into her bathroom and found it very tidy. If Nick had not borrowed one of her huge white bathsheets she wouldn't have know he had ever used the room, except for the water splashes on the floor and walls of the shower cabinet. He must have walked across to his own apartment wrapped in the towel, carrying his clothes, but then there would be nobody up here on this floor to see him. The women who cleaned the apartments never arrived before nine in the morning, when both Gina and Nick had always left for work.

Gina took a long, hot bath, then dressed in a cream crêpe de Chine blouse, a cream sweater over that, and a chocolate-brown straight skirt. She wanted to look capable and cool, but somehow the tightness of the sweater and the elegant little skirt made the curves of her figure more female and pronounced. She bit her lip, hesitating, but didn't have the energy to change again, so, pale and dark-eyed, she went to work. When she walked into the office, she was tense with nerves.

Hazel looked round at her and grinned. 'You're here early! If you wanted to catch Nick, he's already gone.'

She stared blankly. 'Gone? Where?'

'Westminster. He just came in to the office to collect some documents, then he rushed off to have a working breakfast with Lord Trendall. They're discussing that bill the Government plan to bring in to put a muzzle on the Press.'

'Not before time,' Gina said absently, sitting down at her desk. That was why he had left so early! He might have told her. But of course he wouldn't. He had wanted her to sweat and worry and come to work in a state of nerves. Nick was good at this, he was an old hand at war games, and he meant to win.

Hazel was giggling. 'Better not let our Mr Caspian hear you say that!'

Gina stared at her in blank bewilderment, flushing. 'What?'

'You said the Press should be muzzled!' reminded Hazel. 'I don't disagree, they really are the limit sometimes—but I don't think our owner would agree with you.'

'He isn't our owner!' Gina snapped, her green eyes violent.

'Sorry!' Hazel gave her a dry look.

'He may have the majority of the board on his side, but he doesn't own a controlling interest!' Gina knew she was over-reacting, Hazel was giving her a very funny look, but she couldn't help it. It made her so angry to hear Nick described as her 'owner'. He would love it, of course; she could just imagine how he would look if he had been here and heard what Hazel said. Nick had a deeply acquisitive, possessive instinct, but Gina was never going to become one of his possessions.

'OK, I used the wrong word—but he still wouldn't like it if he heard you approving of a new law to muzzle the Press!' Hazel said, and, calming down, Gina smiled rather tremulously at her.

'No, you're right, he wouldn't, but I still think that if we won't put our own house in order and stop invading people's privacy, printing cheap gossip without checking that it's true, or caring who it hurts, even if it is the truth—then sooner or later the people are going to demand that the law gives them some protection against the Press.'

The phone rang as she finished; and, pulling a face, Hazel answered it.

'Hello, this is Mr Caspian's office...no, he isn't here.' She listened, her face intent. 'I see. Yes, I'll tell him as soon as he gets back—he should be back mid-morning at the latest.'

She hung up. 'Dougie Brown from the printing works,' she told Gina, making a note on her message pad. 'He put the redundancy notice up on the board first thing, and apparently all hell broke loose when the men read it. You know Dougie, steady as a rock and no imagination, but he sounded really worried. I hope we aren't sliding back into the bad old Fleet Street days.'

Dragging her thoughts back to the mundane present, Gina frowned. 'You can't blame the men. It isn't easy to find yourself out of a job at Christmas-time.'

'No,' agreed Hazel, eyes sober.

'I tried to persuade him to let natural wastage take its course,' Gina said, 'or at least wait until the New Year, but he wouldn't listen to me. It's true, we do need to cut costs somewhere—and the experts have told him we're still overmanned in the printing works, which made it a natural place to make cuts, so Nick is acting on their advice immediately. I was expecting trouble.'

With Nick Caspian, you were wise if you always expected trouble, because that was what you usually got.

Nick arrived while they were having coffee, his grey eyes flashing to Gina at once, glittering, brilliant, unnerving.

That look was like a possessive hand on her, and Gina felt scalding colour sweep up her face and looked away, hoping Hazel wouldn't notice, but Hazel was too busy reading out the messages which had come in for Nick while he was at Westminster.

'And Dougie Brown rang...there's trouble down in the printing works.'

His face sharpened, his eyes hard points of light in the shadowed thought of his face. 'Did Dougie say what was going on?'

'The men don't like the latest redundancy notice,' Gina risked saying—deliberately using a trace of irony.

Nick gave her a narrow look, then turned back to Hazel.

'Get Dougie on the phone!'

He walked into his own office, Hazel dialled the printing works' number, and a few moments later they heard Nick's voice; loud and angry. Gina distinctly heard him swear, a harsh angry sound which made her flinch.

Hazel raised her brows at Gina without saying anything. A moment later, Nick hung up, walked in to their office and said brusquely, 'If I'm wanted, I'll be in the works,' then he was gone like a whirlwind, slamming doors, making papers rustle and fly off desks.

Gina was deeply relieved that something urgent should have come up just at that juncture, distracting Nick's attention from her, while at the same time she was disturbed at the deteriorating atmosphere at Barbary Wharf.

When they had first moved down to the riverside, she had thought that such problems were a thing of the past, left behind when they left Fleet Street and the old-fashioned methods of craft printing. Nick was paying the electricians who operated the new technology very high salaries. There were far fewer men working in the printing works; he could afford to pay good money. Working conditions were much better too. The men didn't have to work so hard, they didn't become filthy with oil and printers' ink, they weren't working in the heat and sweat of the old printing works in Fleet Street where men got so hot that whenever they could they rushed out to drink pints of beer.

There had been little trouble since they moved into Barbary Wharf, but with a worsening of the recession in Britain and Europe in general Nick had been forced to make cuts in the number of staff in all departments. Nobody liked it, but with advertising revenue and sales down there was an urgent need to cut costs, and staff salaries were an obvious place to start.

There had already been some cuts in the printing works, but now that they had been working at Barbary Wharf for a year it had been possible to evaluate just how many men were needed to run the printing process, and a time and motion study had shown conclusively that they were still employing too many men in that department.

The board had been rather wary of making further cuts, afraid of the men's reactions, but Nick was determined to run the *Sentinel* in the most cost-efficient way possible.

He was stubborn in his pursuit of business efficiency; it was a sort of religion with him. He wouldn't be put off by opposition or hostility. Nick merely became more tenacious and determined when he found his will opposed, as Gina had learnt to her cost.

She and the other directors had lost their battle. She had known that the notice was being pinned to the board that morning, and had been anxious about what might happen next, but last night had blotted everything else from her mind.

Nick came back an hour later, striding into the room, his face locked in a grim and taciturn expression.

'Call a board meeting for the earliest possible time,' he told Gina, and there was nothing personal in his glance, his manner. They might have been strangers.

She was glad about that, yet inconsistently she felt as if he had slapped her in the face.

With hardly a pause, he turned those hard eyes to his secretary. 'Hazel, cancel all my appointments for today and get the heads of departments up here right away, or as near as dammit.'

They sat and stared at him, for a second, and he flared up harshly. 'Get on with it! We're in a state of emergency—we haven't got all day to wait while you two get your wits working!'

The door slammed. Hazel whistled, opening her telephone book. 'This is not going to be an easy day!'

Gina picked up her phone without a word. It had been a lot easier than she had anticipated before she got here. This threatened strike was pure luck, for her. It would keep Nick concentrating on other things, and make her life a lot less difficult for a while.

Hazel's prediction was spot-on, though. The rest of the day, and the one that followed, had been confused and hectic. The meetings in the boardroom went on for hour after hour; sandwiches and drinks were taken in there at intervals, men came and went, grim and frowning.

The board of directors sat gloomily around the long, polished table under the portrait of Zachariah Caspian, arguing with Nick, listening to advice from a series of work study advisors and efficiency experts, trying to make up their minds what to do next.

Then Nick and Gina and Sean Yates, the managing director, saw the leaders of the electricians from the printing works. They were in an angry mood, and demanded to see the list of men who were to be made redundant, then insisted on being told precisely why they were no longer needed after working there for a year. Nick had to fight his case name by name, man by man, and made little headway. The leaders were not impressed by talk of efficiency experts and kept coming back to the fact that it was almost Christmas and this talk of sacking men had come out of the blue without any consultation with them.

'Perhaps we should form a committee to discuss possibilities, explore the whole area of manning and cost-efficiency. We might all come up with fresh ideas, and while the discussions are going on any decisions could be delayed,' suggested Gina.

Nick gave her a furious look. 'We've had expert opinion on what should be done; we don't need any more talking—committees are a waste of time and energy, in my experience.'

The men exchanged looks, then turned their eyes on Gina.

'I think Mrs Tyrrell has come up with a very good idea,' their leader said slowly. 'If we have representation on this committee we might go for that. I have to consult my fellow workers, of course.'

The meeting broke up, and the men all filed out, leaving Nick and Gina alone in the boardroom. Nick turned his angry grey eyes on her.

'What on earth possessed you to put up that crazy idea? Of course they jumped at it—well, they would; it means that they can delay redundancies for as long as they can keep this committee in business, and knowing the way they can talk that could be for a year. I could kill you, Gina. What made you do it?'

'It seemed like a good idea,' she muttered.

He came closer and caught her face between his hands, staring down into her green eyes.

'You did it out of malice, didn't you, Gina?'

She drew a sharp breath, shaking her head, her russet hair stinging his hands.

His fingers pressed into her bones, along the elegant line of her temples and cheeks. 'Yes, that's why, isn't it? Pure spite, because of last night, because you finally cracked and you don't know whether to hate me or yourself for that.'

'I was just trying to stop a strike,' she protested, out-staring him. 'And I did, didn't I? It may delay the re-dundancies but it will help management-worker relations, and save money into the bargain because if they had gone on strike the paper would have lost millions we can't afford to lose right at this moment.'

'Tell yourself lies, if you like,' Nick said coldly. 'You don't fool me. I knew in your bedroom this morning, when you pretended to be asleep... I'd been expecting it, that you would hate yourself in the morning——'

Her skin burned. 'Sorry to be so predictable!' She tried to push him away, her hands flattened on his shoulders.

Nick stood, solid as a tank, still holding her face beween his warm palms, staring down into it with eyes that hunted over her features, looking for the weaknesses in her, for ways of defeating her.

'You wanted me last night,' he bit out. 'As much as I wanted you. It was terrific between us, the best sex I ever had.'

'Shut up!' she broke out, her face so hot that she felt feverish.

Nick looked at her impatiently. 'I'm not ashamed of it, even if you are! We're both adults, we don't have to ask anyone's permission or apologise to anyone. Gina, can't you see what you're doing to me, to yourself? Is that the revenge you want—to drive me out of my mind? Because you're doing a very good job of it at the moment, but it may end up with you destroying the *Sentinel* along with me. Has that ever occurred to you? It hasn't been easy for me to concentrate on this union trouble while half my mind has been obsessed with you.

One day I may make a really cataclysmic mistake because I can't think about anything but you.'

'You never spared me a single thought all day!' she contemptuously told him.

Nick's hands tightened on her face, pressing inwards, hurting. 'I wish that were true! But it isn't. You were on my mind every second of the day.'

'You're hurting! Are you trying to crush me to death?' she whispered.

'Don't tempt me!' he growled, deep in his throat, then laughed with a wild angry amusement. 'I take that back. Do tempt me.' His head bent, his eyes enormous, glittering, mesmeric. 'Tempt me, Gina...'

She shook her head dumbly; she couldn't breathe, her body icy and shuddering.

His mouth took hers fiercely, bruising the softness of her flesh and she hung between his hands, trembling.

Somebody opened the boardroom door. 'Oh, sorry...' Hazel's voice said, half laughing, half embarrassed, then the door slammed.

Nick lifted his head, his eyes closed, breathing thickly. 'What was that?'

'Hazel,' she huskily whispered, flushed and distressed. 'She saw...what on earth must she think...?'

'Who cares what she thinks?' Nick muttered, scowling. 'She would have to walk in at that moment...but I suppose we were bound to be interrupted; this wasn't the time or the place.'

'Nowhere is, and it never will be!' she told him bleakly. 'Let me go, Nick.'

He gave her a bitter, charged smile. 'Never, Gina. When will you get it through your head? You belong to me; I'll never let you go, any more than I'll give up the *Sentinel*.'

But his hands opened and she was free, and Gina ran out without looking back.

There was another board meeting next day, at which her proposal for a committee to study redundancies and working methods was voted on and passed, and she was asked, by the men's representatives, to head the committee.

'We trust you to be fair and honest with us, Mrs Tyrrell,' they said, and she was touched by that.

She accepted quietly, aware of Nick's cynical, hostile stare. Only as the meeting broke up did he halt by her chair and murmur in a low, barely audible voice, 'More power, Gina? You're becoming quite a threat to me. I'll have to watch you.'

She almost snapped back at him, but Nick was looking weary, rather drained. Watching him, Gina felt a strange mixture of emotions; concern for the lines around his eyes and mouth, the pallor of his drawn face, and a stabbing anxiety because now that he wasn't totally absorbed in work he might turn his attention to her again.

Her luck had held, though. Only a day later, Nick had had a phone call from Luxembourg, summoning him there, and had left for the airport as soon as he had rearranged his schedule for the next couple of days...

Staring out at the falling snow which was fast blanketing the winter-bound city, Gina shivered now. He would be back, though, and their struggle for power would begin again. Sometimes she was very tired of it, she wished she could just walk away from the *Sentinel* and the legacy the Tyrrells had left her, her dead husband and the old man, Sir George—all the memories which held her captive and made it impossible for her to give in to the way she felt about Nick Caspian.

CHAPTER SEVEN

ANDREAS KIRK took Sophie to a small, intimate restaurant above a public house in the City of London. She had never heard of it, and was rather dubious when she got out of the taxi and found herself in a narrow, empty alleyway. Around them the city streets lay dark and silent. When all the banks and financial institutions closed for the night the City of London emptied: a tide of people ebbed out into the suburbs each evening and flowed back in again each morning. Few people lived inside the boundaries of the old City.

'The restaurant is up these stairs, at the side,' Andreas said as she rather uncertainly turned towards the saloon-bar door of the pub. Through the grimy leaded windows a little light showed but it barely penetrated the shadows around the pub and Sophie nervously wondered what sort of people were regulars there. She had an uneasy feeling she could guess.

'Are you sure it's open? It doesn't look very open,' she said, poised to make a dash for it in a crisis.

'It's open, and we were lucky to get a booking on a Friday night,' Andreas said with a smile. 'This place is often booked for months ahead, especially at weekends.'

'Have you been here before?' Sophie said, still hanging back at the bottom of the stairs which led to the upper floor of the pub.

'Often,' he said, and obviously knew his way around the place because he flicked down a switch and the dark, narrow stairs were suddenly well lit.

Sophie went up a stair at a time, listening to the increasing buzz of voices from the top floor. Andreas was clearly right. It was crowded. She opened the door and found herself in a shadowy room lit with candles and the flicker of firelight. Sophie stopped dead, and pale, candle-lit faces turned to stare at her from every table, the chatter of voices hushed.

A waiter hurried towards them and then the voices started up again. 'Good evening, Mr Kirk, your usual table, of course. May I take your coat, madam? Yours, Mr Kirk?'

They made their way to a corner table, close to a great roaring log fire which almost filled the massive stone fireplace taking up most of one wall. The waiter brought champagne in an ice-bucket, eased out the cork, filled two fluted glasses.

Andreas leaned over the table, his face carved into strange shapes by the candle-light, and lifted his glass towards Sophie. 'To our better acquaintance.'

She smiled and toasted him back, sipped the dry, bubbly wine. It was very good champagne, she noted; he had expensive tastes, Andreas Kirk.

'If I may suggest . . . they do know how to cook fish here,' he said as they studied their menus. 'The fish is always fresh, usually caught the same day.'

Sophie closed her menu. 'I like fish—you choose; I'm sure I'll like whatever you decide on.'

He drily considered her. 'Do you always let men choose your food? A risky habit, if I may say so. However . . . how do you feel about a fish and tomato soup followed by sea bass cooked with ginger and spring onions? Happy with that? Good, now . . . wine . . .'

The waiter arrived and they ordered, then Andreas leaned back and sipped more champagne, watching her through half-closed eyes. 'Now, tell me about yourself, Sophie.'

'I'm very boring.'

'Let me be the judge of that!' he said with an amiable arrogance that irritated her.

'Not just a barrister, then!' she said tartly. 'A judge too!'

He smiled lazily. 'Start with your family...your parents...'

She didn't intend to tell him much about herself, but somehow Andreas Kirk managed to make her talk. His eyes were hypnotic, or maybe he just asked the right questions. Anyway, Sophie found herself talking away, telling him about Uncle Theo and her father and mother and the rest of the family. He listened as if fascinated. Their soup arrived, hot and spicy, with scraps of torn basil leaves floating on top.

It was delicious. 'I've never tasted anything like it,' Sophie said. 'I must come to this place again.'

'With me, I hope,' Andreas said and she flushed and laughed.

'I wasn't fishing for a second invitation!'

The waiter took their soup plates away and there was an awkward little silence.

'Tell me about yourself,' Sophie rather desperately said.

He gave her a brief glance out of those hooded eyes. 'I'm an enigma,' he said, mocking himself. 'And I prefer to stay that way.'

That was what she was afraid of, and as if to underline his enigmatic status someone came up to their table at that moment, a very big man in a well-cut suit which had a rather old-fashioned air.

'Hello, Andreas, long time no see,' he said in a faintly hoarse voice.

Andreas glanced up, and Sophie picked up a hint of surprise in his face. He smiled, though, his mouth a little crooked. 'Well, hello, Harry. When did you get back?'

'Last week. Thanks for everything you done for my mum, she's been singing your praises ever since I got home.'

'Not at all, I admire your mother very much,' Andreas said, studying him. 'How are you, Harry? Health OK?'

'Can't grumble, considering.' He turned his eyes on Sophie and gave her a long, admiring look. 'Where's my manners? Sorry to interrupt, lady, I hope I haven't spoilt your evening, I just wanted to have a word with Andreas; haven't seen him for eight years. I'll push off now, though.'

She smiled at him. 'That's OK, don't worry about it.'

He went on staring for a minute, then said to Andreas, 'You want to nab that one, she's the real item. Lovely face, lovely nature. Don't get many like her on the market. I'd change places with you any day of the week.'

Sophie blushed but laughed because there was something so direct and almost boyish about the big man.

Andreas glanced at her, then back at Harry. Gravely, he said, 'I agree with you. Nice to see you, Harry. Look after yourself, and, if you can't, give me a ring.'

'Thanks, Andreas.' Harry gave Sophie a clumsy little bow. 'A real pleasure to meet you, lady. Enjoy the rest of your dinner.'

She murmured something and then he was gone, moving lightly for all of his height and weight.

Andreas gave her a wry smile. 'One of my regular clients.'

'I gathered that. He seemed nice, though.'

'When he's sober he can be a pet lamb,' agreed Andreas. 'It's when he drinks that he gets into trouble. He wrapped a policeman round a lamp-post last time. He was lucky to get out in eight years—he was sent down for twelve.'

Their main course arrived and as they began to eat the fish Andreas said, 'Let's forget about Harry; tell me how you get on with your boss. Guy Faulkner, isn't it? I've heard of him, something of a whizz-kid. What sort of guy is he? Clever? Shrewd?'

'Both,' she said, and told him how Guy had transferred from journalism to the law, and how successful he had been so far. 'He's exceptionally good at his job. He really knows the law as it relates to newspapers; he made that his specialist subject, he did his thesis on it— a serious study of newspaper legislation.'

Andreas Kirk listened, eating his lightly grilled sea bass marinated in ginger and spring onions and served with mushrooms and a delicious salad of raw, crisp green vegetables.

'And in character?' he asked when she had stopped talking. 'What is he like as a man?'

A little flush rose in her face. 'He's tough to work for, he doesn't suffer fools gladly and he likes his own way.'

'Don't we all? Is he ambitious?'

'Very.' Sophie was beginning to wonder if Andreas was interested in her—or in Guy! They had been talking about him for quite a while now, and Andreas Kirk showed far more curiosity about Guy than he had about her.

'Which barristers do you use in libel suits?' he enquired and she blinked.

'Well, that depends . . .'

'On what?'

'On who is free and who Guy decides would be most likely to win the case.'

'But who would he call first?'

Sophie looked hard at him. 'Why all the questions? Why are you so interested?'

'Professional curiosity,' he told her with a smile she had to admit was charming. 'Added to the fact that the law is the only thing we have in common, until I can uncover something else!'

Sophie laughed and he grinned at her across the table, the candle-light reflected in his eyes.

'If I was determined to find out I only have to check back on the records, you know. I wouldn't need to pump you for the information. If it bothers you to talk about your job, let's talk about something else, by all means.'

'No, it doesn't bother me,' she said, recognising that what he had said was true. It was a matter of public record which barristers the *Sentinel* used when it had to fight a lawsuit. She mentioned several names, and

Andreas Kirk nodded his recognition of them, said what he thought of their court manner, made gentle fun of one, admired the technique of another. He made Sophie laugh and as he refilled her glass and the meal progressed she relaxed more and more, enjoying his company.

From time to time she noticed that Andreas had caught someone's eye across the room; he smiled, waved, nodded to a number of the tables in response to greetings. Obviously he was well known here, and she couldn't help wondering if all these people were criminals, like Harry. Some of them looked as if they might be—others were very respectable in appearance.

At another time the thought that she was in a haunt of criminals might have worried her, but by then she was past caring. The wine had made her reckless and she was enjoying herself.

'This is a very unusual restaurant,' she said, gazing around at the oak-panelled walls, the ornate plasterwork on the ceiling, heavy with cherubs and elaborate wreaths of flowers and leaves. Red velvet curtains at the windows hung to the floor, shutting out the winter night, keeping the heat of the fire in the room.

The sound of the flames, the warmth, the golden flicker of candle-light, had a soporific effect. Sophie began to be very sleepy, or was that the wine?

On the way back to her flat, in another taxi, she almost fell asleep against Andreas Kirk's shoulder, waking with a start as the taxi went over a bump in the road.

'Sorry. . .'

'It's getting late, and I think we may have had a glass too much wine,' he said cheerfully as the taxi pulled up outside her flat. He helped her out and she stiffened, hoping he wasn't going to try to insist on coming in with her. But he merely took her hand and kissed it.

'Thank you for being with me tonight, Sophie,' he said softly. 'I hope you enjoyed it half as much as I did.'

'It was a lovely evening,' she said, and meant it.

'Then may I see you again?'

Sophie laughed a little shyly, flushed, stammered: 'W-well, yes, I suppose so...' She had meant to say no to another invitation. She wasn't sure why she had ended up saying yes.

Next morning she was shopping in her local supermarket when she walked into Tom Birny doing his own weekend shopping. He was even more casually dressed than usual, in army surplus gear—a camouflage jacket with huge front pockets, loose khaki trousers fastened at the ankles with bicycle clips, a khaki T-shirt over which he wore a khaki sweater.

'Going to war—or the jungle?' she teased and he grinned.

'Checking prices on these soap powders, actually.'

'You should be checking whether they're environmentally friendly, too,' she told him, dropping a packet of soap flakes into her basket.

Tom nodded seriously. 'Oh, I do, don't worry.' He peered at her shopping. 'Do you like kiwi fruit? I always feel as if I'm eating a mouse; those furry skins aren't like the outside of fruit at all.'

'Peel them, then.'

'You're so sensible,' Tom lamented. 'Women always are. That's what's so frightening about them.'

'Oh, you're scared of women, are you?' mocked Sophie.

'We all are,' Tom said, still inspecting the contents of her basket. 'You eat a lot of fruit and salad. So do I. It saves cooking and washing-up, doesn't it? And it's good for you into the bargain. What a lot of polish and stuff—I hate housework. I suppose you wouldn't like to come and do mine sometimes? I'd buy you dinner in return.'

'No deal,' she said, amused. 'I only do mine because my mother gave me a guilty conscience about it.'

'Have dinner anyway?' he asked, quick as a whip.

Sophie should have seen that one coming, but she had been thinking about something else. She looked at him wryly. She liked Tom, but he wasn't the man for her and she knew it, any more than Andreas Kirk was. There was no point in dating either of them; she liked them but not enough.

'Please,' he begged, and she couldn't refuse. He looked so pathetic, all dressed up like a soldier and buying lettuce and tomato because he couldn't cook and hated washing-up. Tom was big and husky, over six feet of muscled manhood, and he hadn't grown up yet. Sophie's maternal instinct betrayed her into nodding.

His face lit up. 'That's great! Where would you like to go?'

'I'll cook for us, a Hungarian meal. Do you like goulash?'

'I don't know, I've never eaten it. But I'll try anything once.'

'All right, then. Come to my flat at seven-thirty. You know the address.'

There might be no future in a relationship with either him or Andreas Kirk, but it would keep her mind off Guy, she thought as she began cooking the goulash that afternoon, then she stopped chopping the beef for the stew, her breath catching in shock. Guy? Why had his name come into her head, instead of Gib's? It was Gib she loved, Gib she wanted to forget—not Guy Faulkner.

A slip of the tongue, she told herself. She hadn't meant Guy. She had meant to say Gib.

Very flushed, she began to sear the beef on all sides in a copper-bottomed pan, the smell already delicious. But her mind wasn't on what she was doing; it was in confusion because she knew she was lying to herself. She had barely thought of Gib that week, and when she did remember him it didn't hurt as much any more.

She bit her lip. It didn't hurt at all, if she was honest. Turning away, she took out the beef with a slotted spoon and put it on a hot plate, covered, to keep it warm, then picked up the sliced and chopped vegetables—the peppers, tomatoes, potatoes and onions—and threw them into the hot fat. When they were lightly browned she returned the beef to the pot, added the various spices, the chili powder, the paprika, the garlic and caraway seeds and finally added the stock. A little while before serving the goulash, she would add a few *csipetke*, tiny dumplings always served in soup or stews.

Once the meal was cooking slowly, she sat down with a cup of coffee and stared at nothing, facing some unwelcome home truths.

Somehow, since the night of his engagement party, Gib had faded from her mind, and she bleakly had to admit that Guy had somehow become important to her. She didn't know how.

But she did know! a little voice inside her head insisted. When Guy had come back to her flat and made love to her while she was so miserable over Gib there had been a traumatic shift in her feelings, a transference from one man to the other. Gib was lost to her, and Guy was there. It was that simple.

She leapt up, angrily shaking her head. No! That made her sound crazy, it made her feelings sound unreal, and they weren't. Gib had made her bitterly unhappy because she had loved him. If she hadn't been in love with him he couldn't have hurt her so much.

But she had gone to bed with Guy, and if she hadn't slept with him that had not been her own choice, it had been an intervention of fate. She had wanted to sleep with him.

OK, she thought angrily. OK, I wanted him that night, but it wasn't personal, it was because I was unhappy and lonely and I'd drunk a little too much.

And ever since you've felt frustrated, said that maddening little voice in her head. Ever since that night you have wanted Guy far more than you ever wanted Gib.

I don't even like Guy! she protested.

What has that got to do with it? asked the inner voice.

You can't love a man you don't like! she argued hotly. I liked Gib so much; he was wonderful, his smile was always warm and kind and he was gentle, funny and marvellous company. Guy isn't gentle or kind and he certainly isn't funny. He's as tough as hell and he scares me.

But you want him more every day, said the little voice. You think of him all the time.

He makes me angry, he makes me want to hit him.

He makes you want to go to bed with him, said the little voice.

Burning heat ran up Sophie's face. 'Shut up,' she said aloud. 'Shut up, shut up.' And to make sure the voice didn't go on she began to tidy up her flat, and kept herself busy doing housework until it was time for her to go and have a shower and dress before Tom arrived.

She was ready early, so she fussed around, lighting the candles on the little dinner table set for two, with crystal glasses and flowers in the centre. She turned the lights down with the dinner switch, put a Frank Sinatra disc on the CD player, and stood back to survey the room with satisfaction. It looked great.

Then the doorbell went and she looked at her watch in surprise. Tom was early! She gave her reflection a quick check in the mirror before she opened the door. The flat was very warm, so she had put on a scarlet silk shift dress cut on the simplest lines—very short, with a low, scooped neckline, and tiny frills caping the top of her arms. In her hair she wore a scarlet silk rose which matched the dress and her delicate high-heeled shoes were silver.

She was smiling as she opened the door, but the smile withered as she looked into Guy's face.

He slowly looked her up and down, his blue eyes hardening. 'Expecting someone?'

'Yes,' she said, as he looked past her, into the flat, and saw the candle-lit dinner table set for two, the dimmed lights, heard the soft murmur of Sinatra singing 'Songs for Swinging Lovers'.

'Charming,' he said through his teeth. 'Who's this for? Kirk?'

'Tom Birny, actually.' She tried to sound cool and at her ease, but her nerves were jumping crazily.

Guy's eyes flicked back to her, a dark and angry blue. It was more than anger she saw in his face, though; there was cruelty, a desire to hurt, in the line of his mouth. Something in Guy had changed, or he had always hidden a facet of his nature that had come to the fore now.

'You're seeing both of them?' His voice bit at her. 'How many others have you got on a string? What are you trying to do, forget Gilbey Collingwood by dating every man you meet? It won't work, Sophie. You'll get yourself into trouble and give yourself a reputation you'll regret when you come to your senses. Gilbey Collingwood isn't worth it. Where's your pride? Why can't you just forget the man?'

Very flushed, she lifted her chin and gave him a coldly defiant stare. 'I wish I knew what makes you think you have a right to keep lecturing me! Frankly, I'm sick of it, and of your interference in my affairs. Just tell me what you came here to say, and then go.'

He gave her a smouldering look, his teeth tight, but after a moment's silence told her in a harsh voice, 'I came to tell you Nick Caspian has asked me to fly to Luxembourg at once. I'll be away a couple of days. Cancel all my appointments until further notice; I'll let you know when I'm coming back.'

'You could have left a message on the answering machine in the office,' she coldly said.

'I wish I had.' Guy turned on his heel to walk away and cannoned into someone who was just arriving. He swore under his breath, muttered something incoherent and strode off.

Sophie looked at her Uncle Theo with flushed embarrassment. 'Sorry about that…he was in a temper…'

'So I saw,' Theo Petofi murmured thoughtfully. 'A very angry young man—what have you done to put him in a mood like that?'

'I haven't done anything!' Sophie walked back into her flat and her uncle followed, closing the front door behind him.

He paused to stare at the scene, the dim light, the lit candles on the immaculately laid table, the soft sweet sounds of music in the background.

'Was all this for him?'

'No, it is not; I'm expecting someone else, any minute now.'

Fascinated, Theo Petofi probed deeper. 'Someone male, obviously? And who was the other one, then? A disappointed lover?'

'No, he isn't!' Sophie's face was hot, and she kept it turned away from her uncle, adding reluctantly, because she knew he would go on asking questions until he got an answer, 'That was my boss, Guy Faulkner.'

'Was it, now? Interesting.'

Sophie's heart sank. The last thing she wanted was for Uncle Theo to find Guy interesting; it would mean an endless series of questions. Uncle Theo on the trail of something was as tenacious as a starving cat which smelt a rat.

Sitting down at the table, uninvited, he said, 'Can I taste the wine for you?' She had opened a bottle of red Hungarian wine and left it on the table to breathe in the warm room.

She gave him a look, half impatient, half affectionate. 'You mean you want a glass? Oh, very well. I shan't be drinking much. We can spare you one glass. Pour it yourself.'

Theo did, slowly, watching the red wine shimmer in the candle-light. He lifted the glass to his nose and inhaled. 'Hmm...good year, that one...' He rolled the wine round his mouth before swallowing. 'Tastes of plums...delicious.'

She watched him wryly. He was a large man, very overweight, with white hair fringing a bald crown like a monk's tonsure, his pink face cherubic but his dark eyes cynical and knowing with something of tragedy behind them. Uncle Theo had known fear and loss and pain during his formative years and had never quite shaken them off even though his life had been peaceful and scholarly here in London. Sophie loved him dearly, and knew he loved her, too.

He twirled the stem of his glass between finger and thumb, tilting it, stared into the wine, saying casually, 'So your boss is in love with you. How do you feel about your boss?'

Breathless and furious, Sophie stammered: 'He isn't...I didn't say...and I'm not... He's my boss, that's all. Don't start imagining things. And what are you doing down here, anyway? Did you want something, or were you just being nosy because you saw a strange man arriving?'

Theo Petofi drained his glass and stood up with a dignified air of reproach. 'I'm insulted. I am never nosy.'

Sophie gave a hollow laugh.

'As it happens,' said her uncle, 'I came down to tell you the family have decided to have Christmas here this year.'

'In my flat?' gasped Sophie, appalled.

'Of course not! Upstairs, in my part of the house. The tenants on the top floor are moving out this week, and I haven't let it again yet, so I'll keep it empty until the New Year, to have plenty of room for the whole family to stay.'

'Oh, God,' said Sophie gloomily.

Theo gave her a scolding look. 'You are a very bad girl—your mother spoilt you, your father spoilt you, I spoilt you. You weren't smacked often enough. I shall expect lots of help from you——'

'That's what I was afraid of!'

He ignored the interruption. 'Getting things ready will take us days. I told your mother you would cook the goose this year——'

'Me? I've never cooked a goose in my life, I don't know how!'

'Talk to your mother, she'll tell you how it's done. And I hope you'll talk to her about your boss, who doesn't love you but looks as if he does to me. Girls should tell their mothers everything; that is what mothers are for.'

The doorbell rang and Sophie gave a sigh of relief. 'There's my guest—and, before you ask, he is not in love with me, and I'm not in love with him, he's just a friend coming to dinner, OK?'

'I don't understand your generation,' Theo grumbled, following her to the door. 'What a way to live! Intimate candle-lit dinners with men who are just good friends? What a waste. You should have had that boss of yours to dinner——'

Sophie gave him a pointed look. 'Stop talking about it.' She pulled open the front door and smiled a welcome to Tom, who was carrying a bottle of champagne, which he handed her. 'Hi, Tom, come in...'

Theo was hanging about, waiting for an introduction, while Tom looked politely and curiously at him, so she had no choice.

'This is my Uncle Theo—this is Tom Birny, a crime reporter on the paper.'

They shook hands. 'Crime, eh? That must be an exciting job to do,' said Theo, and Tom made a little face.

'A bit too exciting, sometimes.'

'Really? Why is that?' asked Theo happily, preparing to settle down again for hours.

Sophie took his arm before Tom could answer him. 'You were just leaving, remember? See you tomorrow.'

Reluctantly, Theo left and Tom gave her a grin. 'Nice old boy, isn't he? He's the Hungarian one? Didn't you say he was a historian? He looks clever.'

'He is,' said Sophie grimly. Uncle Theo was much too clever, that was the trouble. She wished he had not come down in time to meet Guy. She did not want him taking an interest in her private life. He might tell her mother what he suspected and then there would be an inquisition and excited daydreaming about weddings and honeymoons, and Sophie really could not stand much more.

Gina Tyrrell got a phone call from Sir Dermot Gaskell that Saturday, asking her to have dinner with him. 'I've got a proposition to put to you, Gina,' he said, and her antennae prickled warningly.

'I'm always happy to see you, but I'm not getting involved in one of your plots against Caspian International, Dermot!'

'Does he own you lock, stock and barrel now?' sneered Sir Dermot, and she angrily felt her skin redden, glad he could not see her.

'No, he does not! But I detest back-stairs conspiracy. I'll fight him, in my own good time, but I'll do it out in the open.'

'Well, I'm glad to hear you're ready to stand up to him. You must have noticed that a number of board members are losing patience with the way he's running the paper. This recent trouble, for instance, with the print workers—quite unnecessary, very badly handled. He could have avoided confrontation, I thought we had moved on from that era of labour relations, but he seems to enjoy locking horns with the men. A serious strike was narrowly averted, but not by Nick Caspian—by you, Gina. And may I say how much I admire your handling of the situation? It's clear you had the men eating out of your hand. I think you are becoming a real force on the board, and a focus of loyalty for the staff. Sir George would have been proud of you.'

Gina was startled and touched. 'Why, thank you, Dermot, that's very nice of you.'

'I mean every word of it, and it wasn't just me who was struck by the way you handled the print workers. Look, cards-on-the-table time, Gina . . . a number of us have got together and are having talks about our reservations, our lack of confidence in Nick Caspian's judgement. He may be very successful in Europe, but he doesn't seem to understand the British situation at all. I'm sure you agree about that. Anyway, in discussions about a possible change of management, your name came up—certain people thought that you were the natural choice, as a Tyrrell . . .'

'By marriage only,' she reminded him, slightly dazed by what he was saying.

'Ah, but the old man was grooming you to take over when he went. We all know that, and Sir George was a good judge of management material. If he thought you could run the *Sentinel*, he was probably right. If you don't feel you can get involved, we respect your feelings, and for the moment I won't ask you to join us, but...purely as a hypothetical question, say...if we came back to you later and asked you to take over as chairman . . . would you accept?'

'Nick Caspian would never agree!'

'He wouldn't need to if you and Philip Slade joined forces——'

'Philip! Is he involved in this? But he's in the States, he won't be back in London for another week.'

Sir Dermot was amused. 'Well, my dear, there is this modern invention called a telephone . . .'

'You talked to Philip on the phone, and he agreed to back you against Nick?'

'In principle, yes—and a growing number of fellow directors agree with me, I'm happy to say. With you and Philip and a few other shareholders, opposing him, and the rest of the board backing you, Caspian can be voted down so often that he'll be forced to resign. His position would become untenable. He wouldn't have a majority of the voting shares, and without support on the board he couldn't run the paper. You would take over from him.'

Gina turned pale with a strange sort of shock. It was what she wanted . . . wasn't it? So why did she feel so odd now that it might actually happen? 'But . . . me, take over? I don't know if I could, Dermot.'

'Of course you could, Gina! Where's your backbone? You stood up to him in the boardroom the other day, and won. And it isn't the first time; you've been fighting him all year, and getting better at it all the time. I think you're ready for power.'

'But arguing a point with him in a board meeting is one thing. Running the entire paper without him is another. He's a highly experienced newspaper man. I still have a lot to learn.' Her legs had turned to jelly. 'The very idea scares me.'

Sir Dermot laughed noisily. 'Silly girl. We'll all help you, don't worry. All we want for the moment is to know we can count on you and your voting shares. Gina, Gina, this is what you've always wanted, your revenge on him for what he did to Sir George. You haven't gone soft on that, have you? You haven't forgotten the way the old man died?'

'No,' Gina said, turning pale and pushing aside all her personal doubts. 'I haven't forgotten anything.' How could she ever forget?

'Then you're with us?' pressed Sir Dermot and she gave a long sigh.

'I suppose so.'

Sir Dermot made a satisfied little noise. 'Good girl. Leave it with me, and I'll be in touch when everything is in place.'

What did that mean? she wondered, frowning. 'Exactly how many other directors are involved?' she asked cagily.

He hesitated, as if reluctant to tell her. 'Well, we almost have a majority, but there are one or two teetering on the borderline. Look, Gina, I must go. Talk to you later.

I'm sure I don't need to tell you not to discuss this conversation with anybody in the meantime, do I?'

She put the phone down and stared at nothing, her face pale and blank. She ought to feel triumphant and excited because at last Nick was going to be challenged, was going to lose his hold on the *Sentinel*. Instead, she felt depressed and confused. When Sir George died it had all seemed so cut and dried, a clear-cut issue of loyalty and betrayal. Now she no longer felt so sure: everything had shifted inside her mind, the borders had blurred, the issues weren't what she had thought they were.

A sigh wrenched her whole body. Her love-hate torment over Nick was weakening her—she no longer knew what she thought, how she felt, what she wanted.

On the Monday morning another shock awaited her in the office. As she walked in, Hazel was just sealing an envelope, and looked up, a mischievous, rueful smile on her face. Taking off her snow-dusted coat, Gina smiled back at her.

'You look wicked—what are you up to?'

Hazel just grinned as she went into Nick's office with the envelope. Gina skimmed through her own mail, standing by Hazel's desk.

'Nice weekend?' Hazel asked as she came back, and Gina shrugged.

'A quiet one, anyway.' The truth was, with Nick away it had been deadly dull, but she refused to think about that. 'You went over to Utrecht to see Piet, didn't you? How was he?'

'On top of the world. He had news for me.' That excited look was back on Hazel's face and Gina studied her curiously.

'Good or bad?'

'Depends how you see it. For us, good.' Hazel paused for effect, her eyes bright. 'Piet has given notice to Caspian International and has bought premises. We're going into business for ourselves, starting in three months' time.'

Gina had known this was coming some time—Hazel and Piet had been talking for months of starting up their own firm—but it was still a shock and it wasn't easy to smile and sound enthusiastic. She tried, however, because Hazel was her friend.

'That's wonderful! It's what you've both wanted for ages—I'm so glad you're going for it at last. Where will you be based?'

Hazel was fooled by the big smile and laughed happily. 'Holland, of course. Piet thinks it is a practical base to choose—from Schiphol Airport you can fly anywhere in the world, and the auto routes are good, too.'

Teasingly, Gina said, 'And, of course, Holland is his country!'

'Yes,' Hazel agreed, smiling. 'He wants to be based there. You can understand why—he's lived all over Europe now, just for months at at time. He says he wants a little stability and permanence in his life and he wants to be back home.'

As she listened, a little frown pleated Gina's forehead when she began to realise what this would mean.

'So, you'll be leaving us, then?'

'I just put my notice on Nick's desk,' Hazel said, nodding.

Gina gave a groan. 'Oh, Hazel. I shall miss you.'

'Me, too,' Hazel said, and gave her a hug.

Gina felt like crying. 'We've worked together so well for years! It isn't going to be easy working with someone else.'

'Nobody's indispensable,' Hazel brightly said, then gave a quavery grin. 'Although, of course, I'd like to think I am. My contract says I must give a month's notice, so that's what I'm giving, although if you can't find a replacement I can always stay on for a week or two.'

'Thanks,' Gina said gratefully. 'You'll have to help me choose someone. It isn't going to be easy to fill your shoes!'

'My feet aren't that big!'

They both giggled stupidly, close to tears. 'Will you look inside the firm, or advertise for someone from outside?' asked Hazel, and Gina shrugged.

'That's up to Nick, of course, but it would be easier if it were someone I knew.'

There was a tap on the door and Sophie Watson walked in with a sheaf of documents from the legal department. 'When Mr Caspian has seen these can you let us have them back at once?' she asked in her cool, clear voice, turning to go.

Gina nodded rather absently, her mind still on what she and Hazel had been talking about, and Sophie walked out again.

Hazel stared after her, eyes narrowed. 'I just had a brilliant idea!'

'What's that?' Gina asked without really listening.

'Sophie,' said Hazel.

'What about her?' Gina answered vaguely, then her eyes widened and sharpened. 'Sophie?' she repeated, and Hazel nodded.

'Sophie! Well, why not? She's efficient, she's smart, she's always elegant and well dressed. She knows how to run an office and she can speak several languages fluently. I think she's the obvious choice.'

'I hadn't even thought of her,' said Gina. 'But you're absolutely right, she would be perfect.'

Hazel gave her a droll look. 'Hey! Not perfect—I'm perfect. But, as I have to go, Sophie could be a good substitute.'

'If she wants the job,' Gina pointed out. 'I think she likes it in the legal department.'

'She may do, but she would like it even more up here; this office is the most important one in the building. Of course she'll want it. For a start, she'd earn far more money. And she'd have more status and a more varied working day. This is far and away the most interesting job on the paper.'

'Yes, you're right, as always,' Gina said, then laughed wryly. 'But what is Guy Faulkner going to say about losing his very capable secretary?'

CHAPTER EIGHT

NICK and Guy Faulkner flew back from Luxembourg late on Tuesday evening, and on Wednesday morning Nick was back at his desk by the time Gina arrived. When she walked into the office Hazel looked up, grimacing and rolling her eyes towards his door.

'I know he's back, I heard him unlocking his apartment door last night,' Gina said quite coolly, taking off her coat and hanging it up. Knowing he was a few feet away again had kept her awake for hours last night. 'How did he take your resignation?'

'He was flatteringly furious!' Hazel drily told her.

'I knew he would be!'

'Piet saw him in Luxembourg yesterday and resigned in person. I knew he felt he should, he thought he owed it to Nick to tell him face to face. Nick seems to think he may be able to talk Piet out of it, but Piet has made up his mind, and he won't change it. Anyway, Nick wants to see you as soon as you get here. Be careful, Gina, he's in a really bad mood this morning.'

'Well, won't that be a change!'

Hazel giggled. 'He has been pretty bad-tempered all year, hasn't he?' There was a wicked look in her eyes. 'I wonder why?'

Gina refused to take the bait. She was assessing herself in the mirror. 'It isn't quite as cold today, is it?' she murmured. 'And no sign of snow so far today, either! This is turning out to be the worst winter I can remember. It's snowed on and off for weeks now.'

Her skin was flushed from the biting wind in the streets, her green eyes bright. She tidied away some wilful strands of russet hair and straightened the lapels of her smooth-fitting tawny suit. The colour was the perfect foil to her hair and made her eyes look as green as a cat's. Well, something was making her face pink and her eyes glitter, anyway. It could be the thought of seeing Nick again any minute now.

As she turned she found Hazel watching her with amusement. Gina's flush deepened; Hazel winked.

Since the day she'd walked in on them and caught Gina in Nick's arms, there had been a curious glint in her eye whenever he was around, or Gina mentioned him. She had kept a discreet silence on the subject, though, for which Gina was grateful.

Hurriedly walking across the office, she tapped on Nick's door. He bit out, 'Come!' as if she were a dog.

Her lips tight, Gina went in; he sat behind his desk, his dark grey striped jacket off, hung over the back of his chair, his maroon silk tie loosened and his collar open, talking in French on the phone. He glanced round, his hard grey eyes observing her, and waved for her to take a seat.

She sat down, trying to look cool, crossed her legs, very conscious of the restless exploration of Nick's eyes. His voice fast and impatient, he went on talking in his curt clipped French, but all the time he was staring at her long, smooth, silk-clad legs.

'No, I won't accept that. No, that won't do, Rossignol. Don't try and fob me off with promises—I want the whole order delivered at once, or the deal is off. You were given a deadline, and you keep to it, or take the consequences. No, that's just an excuse! Of course you could get it there in time; get moving now, don't hang about arguing with me.' A pause, then he said tersely, 'Very well, you've got two days, and then the guillotine comes down.'

He hung up with a resounding crash that must have made the man at the other end deaf in one ear.

Gina tensed as he leaned back in his swivel chair, his slim body relaxed, and put both hands behind his head, surveying her from her bright, burnished head to her elegantly shod slim feet, lingering en route to enjoy the sight of her long legs, rounded hips and the small, high breasts under her chic suit. From the way he stared she felt he realised that she was only wearing a bra and panties under the suit, which was much too tight-fitting for her to wear a shirt under it.

'Hazel said you wanted me,' she quickly said, to distract him.

His brows flickered upwards. 'Oh, she'd noticed that, had she?'

'If you're going to play word games I'm leaving!' Gina furiously snapped.

He gave her a dry, mocking stare, then pushed a gilt-edged rectangle of stiff card towards her.

'I suppose you've had one of these.'

It was an invitation from Philip Slade to a cocktail party at his London home, to meet his fiancée, Suki Tamaki, and some of her family.

'No,' Gina said, putting the card down. 'Well, not so far.'

'But you will!' Nick said oddly, baring his teeth in what she imagined was meant to be a smile.

'I expect so,' she said, baffled by his tone. Surely he wasn't having fun at her expense because Philip was marrying someone else? He couldn't seriously imagine that bothered her? At one time she had wanted him to believe she was interested in Philip, but gradually she had given up pretending.

'I expect so too,' Nick snarled and she started at the anger in his voice.

'What is this all about?' she stammered.

'Tamaki,' he said. 'Slade's fiancée is one of the Tamaki family.'

Then she remembered Philip saying that his fiancée came from a newspaper-owning Japanese American family. 'Yes,' she warily agreed. 'Suki Tamaki. Have you heard of her family? When Philip rang to tell me he was getting engaged to her I thought the name rang a bell, but I forgot to mention it to you.'

'Oh, you did?' Nick said with searing sarcasm. 'Isn't that odd? Of course it's of no importance that Slade is marrying into the Tamaki family! Why should you bother to warn me about that?'

She looked at him uneasily. 'Why all the heavy irony? What are you getting at?' Had he got wind of Dermot's conspiracy, and the fact that she and Philip were involved in it? Sheer panic made Gina's breathing speed up, her heart thud.

'What am I getting at?' He stood up suddenly, and she stiffened, watching him with wide, nervous green eyes. Nick prowled towards her, and stared down into those eyes, searching them for some betraying expression. 'You really don't know?'

'Kn...know what?' she stammered, her nerves leaping at having him so close to her. Had somebody warned him what was afoot? He would still have some supporters among the directors; men he had planted on the board to keep him informed of what was going on, and to vote the way he wanted them to vote. But would Dermot have been stupid enough to approach any of Nick's friends? She would have thought him far too shrewd and subtle.

A wry smile indented Nick's mouth. 'No, I see you don't. Well, I admit that's a relief, but you damned well should!'

'I'm sorry, but I don't know what the hell you're talking about!' she threw back at him, wishing he would move away, because he was doing something drastic to her heartbeat.

'Fortunately for you, I believe you,' he said rather bafflingly, as if he was suddenly not quite so angry.

Gina shook her head in bewilderment. 'Are you going to tell me what you're talking about or shall I just go away and have a private nervous breakdown somewhere quiet and peaceful?'

He gave her a hard grin. 'How many times do I have to tell you to do your homework, find out everything you can about the newspaper industry worldwide, study the tiniest detail in the trade magazines? Keep learning our business, Gina! You must stop thinking in a purely British context. Ours is an international company, and it will grow in the next decade. We're going global. If you want to be part of Caspian International's future you must learn everything you can about our business rivals as well as ourselves and our markets.'

'I've been trying to,' she protested, and Nick looked into her green eyes and smiled crookedly.

'OK, I'm sorry, Gina, I know you have. You've worked like a Trojan this past year—I've watched you and I've been impressed.'

Gina blushed, very moved; Nick rarely praised her and she valued his opinion all the more for that.

She felt a strange, serpentine coiling inside her body: guilt and fear and regret all twisted together at the thought of the plot Sir Dermot was hatching against him and her own part in that.

It made her sick to think how Nick was going to look at her when he finally realised she had betrayed him.

But he had conspired against the old man, she reminded herself! He had betrayed Sir George and brought him to his death—why should he get away with the glittering prize his treachery had brought him? And why on earth should she feel ashamed because she was doing to him what he had done so often to others? Hadn't she told him a year ago that one day she would revenge the old man? Nick could not say she had not warned him.

And yet she still felt unhappy about it...

'Remember the trip we made to California?' he was saying softly, and she started, her lashes flicking down.

How could she forget it? She had learnt so much about him on that trip. What his mother had told her had given her new insights into Nick Caspian, shown her that, if he was hard, ambitious, ruthless, it was because he had been grievously hurt himself, as a child. Nick had spent a lonely, isolated, loveless childhood; it wasn't surprising that he should have grown up tough and remorseless in pursuit of what he wanted.

'You must have heard of the Tamaki family while we were in California,' Nick said. 'The Tamaki group own newspapers all along the West Coast. Our little team didn't have any dealings with them because they aren't interested in selling, only in buying. This girl's father founded the firm around thirty years ago, and they've been very successful. They're a strong, forward-looking group with good finance.' His frown carved deep lines into his forehead. 'I'm not happy about Slade marrying into their family. His shares are much too important to this company and he wouldn't hesitate to use them against me with backing as powerful as that of old Tamaki.'

'But...' Gina was bewildered and disturbed. 'But surely the Tamaki family have no shares in the *Sentinel*...what harm could they do us?'

'I don't know,' Nick said, his grey eyes dark with thought. 'On the face of it, nothing. But my instincts tell me something is going on behind my back, and my instincts are never wrong. I've always been able to sense trouble before it hits me.'

He turned to stare out of the window, frowning; and Gina watched his razor-edged profile and bit her lip. His instincts were amazing. He was right, of course—trouble was about to hit him, but not from the Tamaki family. His enemies were much closer to him; right inside his own company, in this room, standing next to him at this very moment.

Sir Dermot hadn't mentioned the Tamaki family as being part of his conspiracy, and she did not believe he would go into partnership with total outsiders. No, there was no possible way that the Tamakis could interfere in the *Sentinel*. There were no shares on the market for them to buy, except Philip Slade's, and he only owned a few. True, they were important voting shares, and meant that Philip held the balance between her and Nick, making it possible for her to block Nick when she so chose. But by themselves they were not important.

'You're tired,' she said soothingly. 'You keep flying round Europe, stopping off for a couple of days here, a couple of days there—you've had union troubles in London and elsewhere, problems with money—it isn't surprising that you are starting to be a bit paranoid.'

He gave her a furious look, then suddenly laughed. 'Paranoid, am I? Well, maybe there's something in what you say. Talking about problems ... who on earth am I going to replace Hazel with if she goes? Can't you talk her out of it? She wouldn't listen to me.'

'Nick, she would be leaving soon, anyway. You may not have noticed, but she is going to have a baby, which means she's entitled to six months' maternity leave, for a start, and, in any case, she couldn't keep travelling back and forth to Holland to see Piet every weekend once she had had the baby. They would want to be together.'

'I'm hoping to persuade Piet not to go on with this crazy scheme of starting his own firm, though. I need him. I have several projects lined up for him now that the Utrecht printing works is finished.'

Gina gave him a pleading look. 'Nick, don't interfere again—I know you could talk Piet into almost anything, you can be very persuasive when you like...'

'Can I?' he murmured, coming round the desk to lounge close to her chair, his smile mocking. 'I never notice you being easy to persuade!'

She felt a wave of hot colour sweep up her face, and said angrily, 'Don't start flirting with me, Nick! This is serious! Listen to me! Piet has been dreaming for years of having his own firm; don't talk him out of it. Let him go.'

Nick frowned, staring hard at her.

'Please, Nick,' she said softly.

He leaned down towards her, his eyes fixed on her flushed, serious face and for a second Gina almost let him kiss her, then she turned her face away.

'Stop it!'

He straightened, looking furious. 'Well, to hell with you! So, I have to find someone to replace Hazel, in a hurry. I prefer to work with someone I know and can trust, so I suppose I'd better bring one of my secretaries over here from Luxembourg.'

Gina frowned. 'We thought...Hazel and I thought...Sophie Watson would be perfect, actually!'

'Sophie Watson? Who....? Oh, I know her; Guy Faulkner's secretary.' Nick gave Gina a furious, irritated look. 'I suppose you haven't actually appointed her already?'

She gave him a limpid glance, her green eyes all innocence and hurt reproach. 'Of course not. It was just a suggestion. But as I shall have to work with her it would help if it was someone I knew and liked. Although, of course, if you prefer to bring someone in from Caspian International that is your right.'

'Thank you.' His grey eyes flashed like summer lightning.

She ignored the sarcastic tone. 'But there has been a lot of talk about the high number of Caspian International people who have been brought in to replace staff from the Fleet Street days. Instead of Barbary Wharf some people are calling this place the Tower of Babel these days, there are so many nationalities working here.'

'I had heard the joke,' Nick told her without sounding as if it amused him very much. 'And I also know they call me Caspian the Barbarian.'

She couldn't help a giggle. 'Oh, you've heard that?'

'Months ago. I'm sure you think it well deserved.'

She lowered her lashes but watched him through them, half smiling. 'Well...'

He leaned down close to her again and she stiffened in alarm. 'Be careful I don't live up to the name, Gina,' he menaced softly. 'I'm often tempted to barbarism when you drive me to distraction.'

Pulses beat wildly in her throat. Then, to her relief, the intercom buzzed. He ground his teeth audibly, but, after a pause, stretched out his hand and flicked down the switch. 'Yes?' he snapped.

Hazel's voice tinnily said, 'Mr Yates is here.'

Nick made a reluctant face. 'OK, send him in!' He walked round his desk again, saying to Gina, 'I'd forgotten he was coming to see me about the latest drop in circulation. You've seen the figures, I presume? Frankly, they're worrying me. We must have another departmental conference this week, to discuss them.'

Sean appeared, smiling and bland. 'Good morning, Gina, what a beautiful colour you're wearing—you brighten up a rather chilly day!'

'Thank you, Sean, so do you!' she said, on her way to the door.

'Before you go, Gina, one other thing...shouldn't we have a party for Hazel before she leaves?' asked Nick, and she nodded at once.

'Of course. I'll start arranging it. We have a month to make the arrangements. Will you draw up a guest list or shall I ask Hazel to do that?'

'We must have the heads of departments, for form's sake—but apart from that invite all her friends and anyone else the two of you think should be there. We'll have it at the hotel; I suggest a Saturday night. Oh, and of course Piet must be there!'

Gina nodded. 'What about numbers? How many...?'

'I'll leave all that to you.'

Back in her own office, she picked up the telephone and dialled the legal department's number.

'Sophie, could you come up to see me some time this morning? There's something important I want to discuss with you.'

*　　*　　*

Sophie sat on the other side of Gina's desk, an hour later, and stared at her, eyes enormous, apparently struck dumb by the very idea of working with Nick Caspian every day.

'Do you want the job?' Gina asked, not surprised by the other girl's stunned expression. 'You don't have to make a definite decision here and now, but if you're sure you wouldn't be interested it would help if you said so as soon as possible so that we can start looking for someone else.'

'Well ... I ... it's been such a shock!' Sophie said, her usual air of calm completely blown away.

'He doesn't actually eat people,' Hazel promised her with a grin. 'I won't say he's easy to deal with, because he can be difficult, but you've worked for high-powered men before; it can't be simple working for Guy Faulkner, for instance. You would soon get used to Nick's ways, and he can be a very generous boss. You would earn far more, you'll have more status and influence, and the work is varied and fascinating.'

She started to explain the work in more detail and Sophie listened intently, her face serious. 'And of course I would stay on to train you for a week or so,' Hazel ended. 'I've given a month's notice, but I don't mind staying on for an extra week, if needed.'

'Well, what do you think?' Gina asked, and Sophie looked at her hesitantly, biting her lip.

'Can I have some time to think it over? I think I would like the job, but I would like at least a couple of days' breathing-space before I have to give a definite answer.'

'Of course—we have rather sprung it on you. Let us know by the end of working hours on Friday,' said Gina, and Sophie left, promising to do so.

When she got back to her own office she found Guy looking through the shelves of hefty, leather-bound law books, pulling out first one and then another, skimming through them in search of some piece of esoteric case law, no doubt.

Sophie looked at her watch, hesitating. Guy glanced at her and she said huskily, 'It's almost lunchtime; can I have half an hour extra today? I want to go up West, Christmas shopping. I'll stay half an hour later than usual this evening, to make up the time.'

He nodded, his eyes turning back to the open book in his hand, and Sophie resented his indifference. Though it made it easier for her to tell him what she had to tell him. In fact, she would enjoy it. Let him nod indifferently over this news!

'By the way Hazel van Leyden is leaving her job,' she said offhandedly as she put on her winter coat and buttoned it. 'And I've been asked to take over from her.'

There was a silence that made her blood run cold. She was reluctant to turn round but she couldn't stand in the corner forever, so she slowly turned and across the room saw Guy standing there like a pillar of salt, his face a hard, sculptured mask without expression. Until she looked into his eyes and her breathing almost stopped.

'You've accepted?' he asked, his lips barely parting.

Sophie found it hard to get her reply out; her mouth was so dry. 'I said I'd think about it——'

He took a step towards her, but as he moved there was a brisk knock on the door, it opened, and there was Valerie Knight looking a million dollars in a tight white dress which showed off every inch of her curvy figure.

'Oh, you're here, Guy, good,' she said breathlessly, apparently blind to Sophie's presence, as usual.

'Hello, Val,' he said, and the hard tension in his face dissolved into a smile. Sophie watched them, her teeth tight. It was obvious that he hadn't got over Valerie; look at the way he was staring at her. That dress was meant to make men stare, of course. Valerie knew what effect it had—she loved to see men's jaws drop as she swayed past.

'Colette just had a brilliant idea,' Valerie said excitedly. 'We're going to bring Molly Green and her baby

up to London to do some Christmas shopping; it'll make
a great picture story. But Colette thought I ought to check
with you first, in case a story might cause legal
complications.'

'I don't see why it should,' Guy slowly said. 'Especially if it is largely a picture story. How old is the
baby now?'

'Around three months, and she's gorgeous. She's going
to look just like her mother, you can already see that.'

Guy laughed at Valerie's enthusiasm, his eyes warm.
'You've been keeping in touch with them, I see.'

'Unprofessional of me, but somehow Molly and her
baby really matter to me,' Valerie confessed.

Neither of them cared a damn what Sophie did; they
probably didn't even notice when she quietly walked out
and left them alone.

She took the lift down and picked up a cruising taxi
right outside Barbary Wharf. The brief encounter with
Valerie Knight had crystallised everything for her. She
had been hesitating over whether or not to take Hazel's
job and move up to the directorial floor. Now she was
sure what to do. She would accept.

Seeing Guy with Valerie, watching him smiling at the
blonde girl, had made Sophie realise something she
should have suspected long ago. She was in love with
Guy.

She hadn't been, the night he'd rescued her and taken
her home from Gib and Valerie's engagement party. She
had believed then that she was still in love with Gib, but
now she knew she had been falling gradually out of love
over the weeks that led up to that party. Gib had been
dating Valerie steadily all that autumn and into the winter
months. Sophie looked back over that time and saw her
feelings had altered, little by little. By the night of the
engagement party she was almost over it, but that night
there had been one last flare of feeling—a last flame
from a dying fire.

Why hadn't she realised all this before? She feverishly
wondered as she made her way up to Charing Cross Road
to hunt for books for Uncle Theo through the antiquarian bookshops.

She had been blind to her shifting emotions, stupidly
deaf to her own heart. The night Guy took her home
and made love to her she had responded passionately,
and then despised herself next morning, when she was
back to normal. She must already have begun to fall in
love with him, though. Why hadn't she guessed until
now?

The London streets were crammed with shoppers hurrying along, wrapped up against the icy wind; there was
one long traffic jam through Trafalgar Square, and
tempers were getting frayed.

Sophie's taxi driver angrily sounded his horn, banged
his fist on his steering-wheel, swore out of the window
at other drivers and muttered crossly to her. 'This is a
crazy city, a crazy city. The cars are strangling it.
Something's got to be done!'

Sophie automatically murmured, 'Mmm...yes...
absolutely...'

But she wasn't really listening. Dazed and light-
headed, she was beginning to see the fate in store for
her—the anguish of loving a man who didn't love her.
The pain already ached in her breast, and she was dumb
with misery.

It was such a familiar pain, too. She had been through
this before, with Gilbey Collingwood. She had wasted
months of her life on loving him knowing he did not
love her. And here she was again...

It was a pattern; Sophie saw that. Was she endlessly
going to repeat it? Why did she keep falling for the wrong
men?

The taxi dropped her near Cecil Court and she began
to tour the secondhand and antiquarian bookshops in
that vicinity, with no firm idea of what she was looking
for, except that to please Uncle Theo it had to be some-

thing which fitted into his collection of old books. It would soon be Christmas and she still hadn't found exactly the right gift for him.

Her heart wasn't in it today, though. After half an hour she broke off and went into a pub to get a sandwich and a glass of wine. As she sat at a table near the counter to eat her snack, her eyes wandered around the crowded bar. It was a long way from Barbary Wharf, so she didn't expect to see anyone she knew. But she did.

Gib sat in a corner with a girl she had never seen before, a girl with curly brown hair and a heart-shaped face. She and Gib were laughing uproariously, then the girl leaned over and kissed him, throwing her arms around his neck.

Sophie watched, stunned. Gib had always been surrounded by women, he was one of the most popular men on the paper; but from the minute he and Valerie had become a gossip item at Barbary Wharf Gib hadn't been seen around with anyone else.

Until now.

As if sensing that he was being watched, Gib suddenly turned and looked around the room. Sophie was too embarrassed to meet his eyes; she didn't want to talk to him, either. So she got up and ran out of the pub, leaving her meal unfinished.

She would take a taxi up to Liberty's department store to look for a Christmas gift for her mother, who loved the colour and style of the clothes they sold.

As she paused to scan the traffic, though, Gib came out of the pub and caught her arm.

'Why did you dash out like that? I wanted to introduce you to Harriet. Can you spare the time to come back and meet her?'

Sophie stared at him, dumbfounded. Getting her breath back, she asked warily, 'Who is she?'

'My next-door neighbour. Her father's a judge; Ridgeway, you must have heard of him.'

'Yes, of course,' Sophie said slowly. 'Guy often mentions him—he knows the family quite well, I think.'

Gib grimaced. 'That's why I want you to meet her! Harriet met Guy when they were both studying law, they saw a lot of each other for a while, and her father was very keen on the idea of Guy marrying into their family. Guy's family have money, you know.'

'No, I didn't know,' Sophie said through what felt like a mouth full of broken glass. 'I know very little about him.' A wave of bitterness came up inside her. That was an understatement. She had thought she knew him quiet well, but obviously she had been way off.

'Well, thc Faulkners are very wealthy,' said Gib. 'They have land, an estate somewhere or other. And Judge Ridgeway liked the idea of his daughter marrying a rich lawyer. Most of the other guys Harriet met were poor students with a career to build. Her father didn't want her marrying one of them!'

'So Guy has been engaged to her all this time, secretly?' said Sophie in a voice which she held steady only with tremendous effort. 'Isn't he the dark horse?'

'No, you don't understand! Harriet let her father think she and Guy were engaged, and whenever talk of a marriage came up she said she wanted to get established in her career first—but the truth was she was secretly seeing someone else. Someone her father detests like poison. As Harriet says, she *would* have to fall in love with the very last man in the world her father would want her to marry! And she's too scared of her father to dare to tell him. She hasn't even dared tell Guy in case he feels he ought to tell her father, because Guy doesn't have a very high opinion of her man, either.' Gib put an arm round Sophie's waist and smiled down at her. 'She's in a bad way, Sophie—won't you come and meet her? She knows all about you and she's dying to talk to you.'

Warily, she asked, 'What have you told her about me?'

'I barely mentioned you,' Gib said, grinning in a way that made Sophie's colour deepen.

'Guy?' she huskily queried, but Gib shook his head.

'No, not Guy. Oh, she knows you're Guy's secretary, of course, but he hasn't talked about you. Harriet's man told her all about you...'

Sophie's eyes rounded. 'I know him?'

Gib nodded. 'He's joining us here any time—stay and see him. But first come and talk to Harriet; she wants to ask your advice.' He gave her an indulgent little smile. 'She's a darling and a honey and I'm very fond of her, but before she can even brush her teeth she has to have half a dozen opinions on which way and how often!'

Sophie laughed and turned to let him lead her back into the pub, but Gib stopped dead, staring at a tall man hurrying towards them.

'And talk of the devil—here he is!'

'Andreas!' she gasped out, her eyes dilating in shocked disbelief.

'Sophie?' He looked startled, too, although he could not have been as incredulous as she was. She watched him flush and look oddly off balance, and the whole picture suddenly became very clear.

She remembered Andreas, putting question after question about Guy, puzzling her with his interest in her boss, making her faintly suspicious of him and his motives. Her female intuition had told her that Andreas wasn't really interested in her. But she hadn't been able to work out what he was up to!

'So *you* are Harriet's mystery man?'

Andreas gave her a wry, apologetic smile. 'Guilty, I'm afraid!'

'Why didn't you tell me when we had dinner?' she asked bluntly.

'I wanted to get to know you first,' he confessed. 'Have you met Harriet?'

'She saw her with me in the pub,' said Gib, grinning. 'And rushed out with dark suspicions, I'm afraid.'

Sophie drily said, 'You're lucky you caught me, I might have blurted out what I'd seen to Valerie, and then where would you be?'

'Val knows about Harriet,' Gib said cheerfully. 'She's met her a few times. In fact, it was Valerie who advised her to get Guy to break the news to her father.'

Sophie's eyes opened wider. 'You're kidding? She's really going to ask Guy to tell him?'

'He isn't in love with Harriet; he never was,' Andreas quickly said. 'But he is the one man in the world who might make old Ridgeway be reasonable. If Guy Faulkner advises him to make the best of it, the old man probably would.' He made an impatient face, his eyes glinting resentfully. 'I know the old man hates my guts— we have very different views of the law and how it should be practised. He calls me manipulative, but he has to admit I'm successful, and, for all his dislike of my methods, I do operate within the law, I never step outside it. I have criminals for clients, but I'm not one, myself.'

'Come in and meet her,' Gib urged, and Sophie let him lead her back inside the pub to where Harriet Ridgeway was waiting anxiously, her face pale, a half-drunk glass of white wine in front of her.

They shook hands and Harriet said in a warm, husky voice, 'Andreas said you were classy, and I see what he meant now.'

Sophie smiled slightly. 'I'm wondering exactly what you and he were hoping I might do for you...'

Harriet looked helplessly at Andreas, who shrugged.

'Harriet won't let me talk to the old man face to face...'

'He might have a heart attack!' Harriet protested. She gazed at Sophie, her brown eyes huge and childlike. 'So... you see, I thought... please, Sophie, will you tell Guy and ask him to break it to my father?'

CHAPTER NINE

COLETTE TSE tapped her perfect white teeth with a pencil, staring down at the blown-up, glossy photos which were strewn all over her desk.

'Good, aren't they?' said Valerie with satisfaction. 'My favourite is this one, Molly with the baby and a big teddy bear on her lap. Molly's very photogenic, and so is the baby. Oh, we bought the teddy, by the way. Our present to the baby. It's the biggest item on my expenses. I'd no idea toys could cost that much, but we wanted something big and expensive-looking. Deirdre, they call her—the baby, not the teddy! Cute, isn't she?' She moved the picture towards Colette with a fingertip and Colette's almond-shaped eyes flicked over it.

'Not bad,' conceded the features editor without enthusiasm. 'But there's nothing new here, Val. Cute, but we need more than cute. Where's the impact?'

Valerie looked up, eyes sharp. 'I don't know what you mean. This is the perfect Christmas story. Mother and baby... rejected and forlorn at Christmas time... and Molly has that Madonna look...'

Colette gave her a dry look. Her slender, olive-skinned fingers moved gracefully, brushing the photos up into a heap.

'No, sorry, we can't use any of them. It would be a waste of space.'

Valerie was furious. Colette eyed her face sideways, assessing her mood. Ambitious herself, she always knew when one of her staff was ambitious, and that certainly applied to Valerie. Colette didn't fear her, but she didn't want to make an enemy of her, either.

'If you could get Mac Cameron into the frame, it would be different!' she suggested softly.

Valerie gave an angry laugh. 'He wouldn't even see them, let alone agree to be photographed with them!'

'If it was sprung on him...'

'You mean take them along to his flat... and grab a picture before he knows what is going on?' That idea hadn't even occurred to Valerie, and her tone made her opinion of it clear. 'Molly would hate it. If she trusts me, it's because she knows I wouldn't pull a cheap stunt like that.'

Colette's smooth skin darkened with anger. 'You're a reporter, not a social worker,' she snapped. 'Either drop the story altogether, or come up with a more dramatic picture. Just don't waste my time!'

Valerie went down to Torelli's to get a sandwich, brooding over Colette's decision. She was a tough cookie, that woman; she didn't suffer fools gladly and she didn't make any concessions to words like 'ethical' or 'kind'. A story was a story in her book—whoever it hurt!

On her way back, with her lunch in a paper bag, she ran into Gina coming back from a lengthy Christmas shopping expedition, laden with festively printed carrier bags.

'Been busy?' teased Valerie as they waited for the lift together, and Gina nodded.

'Having fun, too. I love buying presents.'

That reminded Valerie of her morning spent with Molly and her baby, and her face tightened. 'Yes,' she said absently. 'Same here.'

Gina noticed. 'Anything wrong? You look fed up!'

'That is the understatement of the century!' said Valerie, and told her what Colette had suggested. 'If she thinks I'm going to be able to talk Molly into going to Mac Cameron's flat and surprising him into a snatch picture, she's out of her skull! Molly would rather die. Sometimes I think Colette doesn't understand human beings at all.'

'Well, it helps if you are one!' Gina said, and Valerie giggled.

'I have often wondered if she was a robot.'

'Nick Caspian probably has hundreds of them in some laboratory in Luxembourg!' said Gina and they both laughed, then Gina said thoughtfully, 'You know Mac has been having a series of tests to establish whether or not he is capable of having a child?'

'Yes, I'd heard, but the results aren't through yet, are they?'

'No, but I'm so sure that that baby is his, aren't you?'

'Absolutely certain!' Valerie gave a little sigh. 'All the same, I shall keep my fingers crossed that those tests back her up.'

'I think they will. Look, Val, what if I invited Mac to my flat for drinks . . . and you brought Molly and the baby along too?'

Valerie gave her a startled, incredulous look. 'You would do that?'

Gina was the last person she had expected would be ready to pull a stunt like that! Colette, yes. Sure. Colette would sell her own granny to get a good story. But not Gina!

Reading her expression, Gina laughed drily. 'Oh, not just to get a picture for the *Sentinel*, no. But to bring Mac and Molly together, in private, where they could talk face to face without lawyers or reporters! It's time they did, don't you think? This has dragged on long enough.'

'Much too long!'

'Then we're agreed?'

Valerie nodded. 'Agreed.'

Gina pulled her diary out of her bag and flicked over the pages, frowning. 'Almost Christmas already. There isn't time. How about December the twenty-first? I'm free that evening, how about you?'

Valerie was looking at her own diary. 'Fine for me.'

'OK, then—leave Mac to me, you get Molly there. Tell her it's a little party for her and the baby; we must have the baby. If she can't make it that day, find out when she can, and ring me at once. As soon as we're sure she can come, I'll invite Mac.'

The lift arrived and they walked into it. Gina dropped a parcel and someone picked it up for her; she gave the man a vivid smile which made him blink.

'What time?' Valerie asked her as the lift shot up.

'Six-thirty? That's cocktail time, and he's usually free at that time of day.'

The lift stopped and everyone else went out. The lift went up again. 'Once we've got them there we can discreetly vanish and leave them alone,' planned Gina. 'I'll say my housekeeper has the evening off, and ask you to come and help me in the kitchen.'

Valerie gave her a dubious look. 'And you think they'll buy that?'

Gina shrugged. 'Probably not, but that doesn't matter.'

'The chances are Mac Cameron will walk out in a rage and never speak to you again, you know.'

'I know.' Gina agreed, not looking very disturbed. 'That's a risk I'll have to take.'

'Maybe I should clear this with the lawyers?' Valerie said uncertainly. 'I could ring Guy and ask what he thinks. He gave me the OK on pictures of Molly and the baby, but this is different. If Mac Cameron turned nasty over this, and demanded money with menaces, my job would be on the line.'

'No,' Gina said firmly. 'He can't sue me for inviting Molly and the baby to my party—don't be silly. But if you tell Guy what I'm planning he might try to stop me, in case it complicates the lawsuit, and I really want to do this. I'm sure Mac loves Molly and that when he sees the baby he'll realise it is his. He isn't happy the way things are at the moment. He desperately wants a child; he just doesn't think he can have one.'

'Maybe we should wait for the results of those tests?'

'And have Molly think he needed proof before he would believe her?' Gina gently murmured. 'No, let him admit he loves her first, and the proof can follow.'

That afternoon she rang Mac, unsurprised to find herself talking to his answering machine, and left a message inviting him to have a Christmas drink with her on the twenty-first of December.

Nick and Hazel were in the other office looking through a pile of folders for any papers which were no longer useful and could be shredded, but as Gina put the phone down she thought she caught a movement in the doorway, out of the corner of her eye.

She looked round, tensing up; but there was nobody there. She must have imagined it.

Mac rang her next morning when she was about to go into a meeting of heads of department. 'Is this a big party, or just the two of us?'

'There will be a few friends there, but not too many,' she said evasively. 'Do try to pop in, Mac.'

'Will Caspian be there?'

'Nick? No, he won't be there!'

A hand came over her shoulder and took the phone away from her. She shot a stunned look up at Nick's hard face and furiously struggled to get the phone back.

He held her off with one hand, without much effort, while he said curtly into the phone, 'Gina's mistaken, Cameron—I will be there!'

'Give me that phone!' seethed Gina.

Nick ignored her, listening intently to Mac. 'I see,' he said at last, his face altering. 'Well, yes, Cameron, in that event, we must talk. I'll see you at the party.'

He hung up and Gina angrily turned on him, her face highly flushed and her green eyes glittering, spitting like a cat. 'How dare you snatch that phone away and tell him you were coming to my party? I didn't invite you, and I don't want you there! You may have ruined everything with your stupid——'

'He's dropped the case,' Nick cut in, and Gina's furious voice died away.

'What?' She stared, eyes stretched.

'Well, that's one piece of good news, anyway,' Nick drawled. 'I only wish he had dropped it before we spent a fortune briefing one of the most expensive barristers in London. I've a good mind to make him pay our costs.'

'Did he say why...?'

Nick shook his head. 'He said he would explain at your party, he was glad I was coming because it would give him a chance to have a private word without the lawyers sitting in on it. No doubt he's hoping to talk me out of any reprisals in the future—he'll be afraid we might give him a very hostile press after this.'

Excitedly, Gina thought aloud, 'It has to be the tests! What else could have made him change his mind?'

Sean Yates put his head round the door. 'Problems?' he queried rather nervously.

'No, good news, for once,' said Nick, walking past him into the boardroom, saying, 'Where's Guy Faulkner? Ah, there you are, Guy—we've got news for you. Cameron is dropping the case—we've won.'

Startled, Guy asked, 'What changed his mind?' just as Gina had, but Nick simply looked enigmatic, smiling sidelong at her.

'We'll find out this evening,' he said.

In fact, Nick was delayed at the office by the arrival of some East European politicians who wanted to be shown around Barbary Wharf. Nick would not normally be expected to be there, but they happened to be paying this visit under the auspices of a member of the House of Commons who was one of Nick's friends.

'I'll see you later, though,' he promised Gina, who sweetly answered,

'Oh, please, just forget the party. I know how busy you are!'

His grey eyes threatened. 'I'll get there, don't worry.'

But she did worry. Nick was taking over her whole life, and she found herself helpless to stop him. He didn't listen to her protests, for one thing, and for another she was paralysed by guilt and anxiety over her own part in Sir Dermot's plot. She was sleeping badly, there were dark shadows under her eyes, but she had to pretend to be full of the Christmas spirit, for Molly Green's sake.

Gina had asked Valerie Knight to bring Molly and her baby a quarter of an hour before she expected Mac Cameron to arrive, but it had begun to snow again and traffic was very bad at that time of day. Mac arrived first, his face lit up as he kissed Gina on both cheeks.

'Happy Christmas, Gina; you look like the fairy on the Christmas tree!'

She laughed. 'I felt glittery this evening!' Her gold silk pleated dress had been just the thing to put her in a party mood.

'It suits you, and I hope this will too!' He produced a package wrapped in scarlet foil, tied with an elaborate gold bow, and she groaned, shaking her head.

'Mac! I wasn't expecting this!'

'It's just some perfume,' he assured her.

'But I haven't got anything for you.'

'I've just been given the best present of my life,' he said as she opened the package and admired the fluted little bottle of French perfume inside.

Gina almost dropped the perfume, her eyes widening with excitement. 'Mac? You've had the results of the tests?'

He nodded, his face flushed and elated. 'It seems I am capable of fathering a child, after all.'

'Oh, Mac, that's wonderful! I'm so happy for you!'

'Thank you,' he said, kissing her again. 'The best thing about that is that I really believe you are, and not just because it lets the *Sentinel* off the hook. You're not a Christmas fairy, Gina, you're an angel.'

She laughed, then sobered. 'But, Mac, why were you ever told you couldn't have a child?'

'They hedged on that one. They said it could be that the tests weren't done properly, or the results misread—but they say it could also be because I have what they call a variable sperm count; some of the time it *is* too low, and if I'd had the test at the wrong time it might have looked as if I was completely unable to father a child. But at times it is more or less normal. It depends on all sorts of factors, whether I'm too hot or too cold, whether I'm tired, if it is early in the morning or late at night. They also said that research is going on all the time and these days it is much easier to help infertile people than it was even ten years ago, when I had my tests.'

Gina nodded, watching him intently. 'Have you spoken to Molly yet?'

He flushed darkly, shook his head, was silent for a second then burst out, 'God, what on earth could I say to her, Gina? I've behaved like a pig, she must hate me by now, and I wouldn't blame her if she does——' He broke off and sighed heavily.

'But you want to see her?' Gina murmured tentatively.

He gave a groan. 'Desperately! But how can I?'

'You haven't even seen your baby yet, have you?'

His eyes were wide and wet. 'No. If only... if I apologise and offer her any terms she likes... do you think... would she let me at least see the baby, do you think, Gina?'

The doorbell went again. 'What's the betting that's Caspian?' Mac muttered, rubbing a hand across his eyes. 'I'm going to have to eat humble pie—will he make me swallow every crumb?'

'Maybe,' Gina said softly. 'Mac, pour yourself a drink.'

'I need one!' he agreed, turning to the drinks table.

Still carrying her perfume, Gina went to the front door. She knew before she opened it that it wasn't Nick ringing the bell.

Valerie met her eyes, her face enquiring.

'Everything OK?'

The cryptic sentence held a dozen questions in one. Her eyes signalled them all. Gina nodded, silently reassuring her; then turned her smile to Molly and the baby, which was half asleep, small face just visible in the white fur hood of her warm snow suit.

'Thank you for coming in this weather,' Gina said. 'It looks as if we're going to have a white Christmas, doesn't it? Never mind, it's very warm in here. Let me take your coat. Shall I hold the baby while you take it off?' She gave her a wry grin. 'That's just an excuse— I'm dying to give her a cuddle!'

Molly handed the baby to her, and Gina rather awkwardly took her, unused to holding babies. She gazed fascinated into the pink face; the blue eyes were drowsy, heavy with sleep, and Gina could see no resemblance to anyone in her features, the eyes, the button nose and bow mouth. As Gina held her she stretched, yawning widely, and they all laughed.

'She's adorable!' Gina said, a deep instinctive wrench inside her. For long acres of time she forgot how much she wanted children, but holding this child now that broody ache came back. Her biological clock was ticking; she was rapidly approaching thirty and each year went faster than the one before.

Valerie had helped Molly to take off her coat. She hung it in the hall closet.

'Was it a difficult journey in the snow? For some reason we never seem to expect snow, and public transport always breaks down at the first sign of a snowflake,' Gina said, her eyes still on the sleepy baby. 'We'll have a car to take you home, don't worry. Are you staying with your parents?'

Molly nodded, running a brush over her dark, windblown hair. 'We live with them; my mother looks after Deirdre while I'm working.' She slid the brush back into her bag. 'My parents have been wonderful——' She broke off, taking a sharp breath, as Mac Cameron appeared from the sitting-room. Molly lost all her colour and put a trembling hand up to her lips.

'Oh...oh...' She looked wildly at Valerie, eyes accusing. 'How could you? I thought I could trust you. You had no right to...you should have told me...' She bit her lip and gave Mac a brief, nervous, flickering glance. 'I didn't know!' she muttered defensively, angrily. 'If they'd told me, I'd never have come!'

Mac was holding a glass of whisky; the ice in it clinked and rattled as he slowly put it down on a nearby table.

'I believe you,' he said huskily, and Molly gave him a disbelieving look, realising now that something was different, that he was looking at her shyly, pleadingly.

'You do?' she whispered.

He nodded. 'I didn't know, either; we were both set up.' He gave an unsteady sort of laugh.

'It seemed like a good idea,' Gina said, but neither of them so much as looked at her. They were too busy staring at each other.

'I've been trying to work up the courage to ask you to see me,' Mac said.

'Have you? What about?' Molly seemed dazed; her skin was flushing pink again, her lips trembling.

'I...oh, Molly, I'm so desperately sorry...'

'Well, we have things to see to in the kitchen, will you excuse us?' said Gina hurriedly, holding out the baby. Molly seemed too dazed to understand what was going on, but she instinctively took her daughter while Mac watched, taking a step closer. The white fur hood fell back, revealing a mass of dark curls, a small face, dark blue eyes.

Mac made a rough, incoherent sound and the baby's eyes slowly turned to stare at him.

Gina and Valerie made themselves scarce. In the kitchen, Gina quickly turned on the radio, a music channel. The latest hit song was playing, and she turned it up to drown any sound from the rest of the flat then she and Valerie made themselves some coffee. They sat and drank it while Gina filled Valerie in with everything Mac had told her.

'At least my job is safe!' said Valerie mundanely, and Gina gave her a wry look.

'The main thing is, Molly and her baby will be fine now!'

Valerie grinned defiantly. 'You don't have to worry about paying the rent and where your next meal is coming from! Us working girls have to be down to earth. I care about Molly, I always liked her—and I fought for her, don't forget that! At the same time, I want to keep my job.'

'I'm sorry, I know you care about Molly,' said Gina apologetically. She had not been too sure she liked Valerie Knight at one time, but she had come to admire and respect her over the last months. Valerie had stuck to her guns, she hadn't ditched Molly and agreed to apologise for having written that story, which would have involved calling Molly a liar—and she had been proved absolutely right.

'I can't wait to tell Gib how Mac looked when he saw the baby!' Valerie thought aloud. 'When you told me Mac Cameron had dropped the suit I picked up the phone and rang Gib to tell him, and he said we would have dinner at the Savoy tonight, to celebrate.'

'Sounds terrific!'

They stayed in the kitchen for twenty minutes, then Gina ventured slowly out. Mac and Molly were quietly sitting close together on a couch, Molly's head on his shoulder, the baby nursed in the crook of Mac's arm. The lights were turned down, just two table lamps glowing; and in the hearth leapt flames which looked quite real but were actually gas-fired, with artificial logs piled up in an ironwork basket.

Gina had spent ages decorating her flat with holly and ivy and glittering foil chains and stars. A large Christmas tree stood in a corner, dripping with silver tinsel and ornaments. She looked at the room with satisfaction and was about to tiptoe back into the kitchen when Mac looked round and went rather red, but smiled at the same time.

'Oh, hello, back again?'

'Everything OK?' Gina asked.

Molly looked round, too, her smile tremulous; she looked as if she had been crying and might still break down again. 'Everything's fine now,' she said huskily.

'I'm so glad, for both of you...' Gina looked at the sleeping baby. 'For all three of you!' she added, laughing.

Valerie came out, grinning, with a tray of hors-d'oeuvres: hot food like tiny *vol au vents* filled with shrimps or chicken in cream sauce, sausage slices in brioche, cheese straws; cold food including thin slices of fish terrine, caviare with chopped onion and chopped hard-boiled egg, cucumber sandwiches. At Valerie's suggestion, Gina had ordered all the food from the Torelli wine bar, and had brought it back when she came home from work that evening.

'Party time!' Valerie cheerfully announced. 'You two haven't got a drink! Come to that, neither have we! So, come on, Mac, hand that baby to her mother, there's champagne on ice in the kitchen, open a bottle, and pour us all a glass.'

Mac and Molly exchanged looks. Mac stood up, still holding the baby in his arm. 'I'm sorry, Gina...we're very grateful to both of you, but all we really want is to be alone to talk about our future. Would you mind very much if we left now? Would it spoil your party? I suppose the others will be along soon, anyway?'

'Yes,' said Gina quickly. 'Any minute. Of course I don't mind if you leave; we understand, don't we, Val? You run along. Have you got your car with you, Mac? Or shall I call for a cab?'

'I've got my car downstairs; we'll be fine. Thanks again, Gina you really are a Christmas fairy, after all— a fairy godmother...'

Molly whispered something indistinct, her lips trembling, Valerie helped her back into her coat and Mac put his arm round her, steering her protectively out of the flat.

When they had gone Valerie gave Gina a wry smile. 'Well, that must be the shortest party on record! It's great to see them so happy, though. Molly was almost light-headed, wasn't she? Didn't know what had hit her.' She looked around the sitting-room. 'Oh, Gina—all this food, and the champagne . . . I'd love to stay and help you out with it all, but would you mind if I hurried away, too? I don't like the look of that snow, it's turned into a positive blizzard and I've got to meet Gib in the Savoy at eight-thirty. If the roads are snowed up it will take me ages from here.'

'That's OK,' Gina assured her, and five minutes later she was alone in the flat with the strange dead silence of snow outside, muffling the sounds of London and giving the night an eerie whiteness.

She looked at her watch. Nearly seven-thirty now. Would Nick still come? Or had he got caught up in some crisis at Barbary Wharf? Or maybe he had been so late leaving the building that he had gone on to dinner somewhere, forgetting that he had said he would come here first?

She picked up a small plate and loaded it with a few of the hors-d'oeuvres, poured herself some orange juice, and sat down on the carpet in front of the fire. She might as well have a private little party of her own.

The doorbell buzzed loudly just as she bit into a small pastry shell filled with spinach and cream cheese. Gina's nerves screamed and she dropped the rest of the pastry; flakes of it sprayed the carpet as she shakily got up.

'Sorry I'm late,' Nick said, his grey eyes slowly drifting down the glitter of her gold silk dress.

'Too late, I'm afraid,' she said, barring his entry. 'The party's over; everyone's gone.'

He shot a glance over her shoulder. 'Is that champagne I see? Just what I need.' He put his arm round her waist and lifted her out of his way, kicking the door shut behind him.

'Nick, one day...' she spluttered, and he grinned down at her, letting her go.

'Yes, Gina...one day...'

Their eyes warred and hers fell, a hot flush stealing up her face. Nick sauntered away, talking casually.

'It wasn't an easy drive home. It was like driving through soup; there was so much snow that my windscreen wipers barely managed to keep going.' He pulled the champagne out of the ice-bucket and wrapped it in the white napkin, took off the foil and began easing the cork out with a practised hand.

Gina picked up two fluted glasses; the cork popped and Nick deftly poured the bubbly wine. He pushed the bottle back into the ice, then took one glass from Gina.

'So, what's the toast?'

'Molly, Mac and their baby,' Gina proposed, and they lifted their glasses and drank some of the chilled dry wine.

'Tell me what happened, then,' Nick said, throwing himself into one corner of the couch in front of the fire.

'Will you have some of this food? Nobody ate any, and there's a ludicrous amount of it. These savoury pastries are very good and so is the caviare.'

'Yes, let's have a champagne picnic in front of your fire,' he said. 'Give me some of everything...I'm starving, I skipped lunch to work on the International accounts. The picture isn't unsatisfactory, as a whole, but one or two countries aren't doing as well as I'd expected; their projected figures for last year certainly weren't matched by the actual profits. I shall have to tighten up the management in the New Year.'

She piled food on to a plate for him, while he went on talking in a tired voice, his body slack and weary on the cushions of the couch. When she brought it over he took the plate with a grin.

'I won't need to eat dinner after all that!'

'You said some of everything!' Gina sat down on the carpet again and picked up her plate. Nick refilled their glasses.

'Now tell me about Cameron and the girl.'

'Molly.'

'Molly,' he nodded, giving her a teasing sideways look through dark lashes.

So Gina talked in between mouthfuls of food, they both sipped champagne and outside the snow blew past the window and London was muffled in an icy blanket.

'A white Christmas,' Gina said with a yawn an hour later. 'That should be fun.'

'What will you do for Christmas?' Nick asked, watching the lazy stretch of her body with darkened eyes. Gina felt him staring and her mouth went dry; she hurried into speech to cover her intense awareness of him.

'Roz and Daniel have asked me to share theirs. Des is flying here tomorrow and Irena and Esteban arrive on the twenty-third. They want to have a real family Christmas, then Irena and Esteban are going back to spend a few days with her mother and brothers after Christmas.'

She started collecting up the rest of the food to take back into the kitchen and Nick got up and helped her. When the sitting-room was tidy again he poured the last of the champagne into their glasses.

'No, I've had enough, thanks,' said Gina. 'What about you? What are your plans for Christmas, Nick?'

'My mother was coming over here for Christmas, but in this weather it might be better if I go to San Francisco,' he said heavily. 'A pity, she was looking forward to seeing you again.'

Gina flushed. 'I would have loved to see her, too.'

He stared into the flames, his face tense. 'Then come with me, Gina. I know Roz has invited you to be with them, but they're obviously having a family get-together; I'm sure you would be welcome, but they won't really miss you.' He drew an audible breath. 'But I would.'

She stiffened, eyes lowered, colour coming and going.

'I want you with me at Christmas, Gina,' he said deeply.

'I can't...Roz has made all the arrangements...'

'Of course you can. She'll understand.'

'I'm sure your mother would rather have you to herself; she sees so little of you.'

'She told me to ask you. She is looking forward to seeing you again. Come on, Gina, don't you want a few days in the sun?'

She wanted to go, badly: to be with him, at Christmastime, to see his mother again, get to know them both better. The temptation was unbearable, but Gina wouldn't let herself give in to it. Sometimes when Nick smiled at her like that her whole body melted and she felt a flood of feeling run through her, but she mustn't forget that Nick was very deceptive, a poker player; that charm of his wasn't worth a spent match. He had lied and cheated before, he would do so again, and only a crazy fool would let herself love him. She knew she couldn't risk spending the holiday with him, in the same house. It was too dangerous.

'No,' she said flatly. 'I can't, I'm sorry.'

Nick realised she meant it. His face hardened, his eyes icy. 'To hell with you, then!' he snarled, getting up. She was afraid for a second, but he strode out, the front door slamming behind him.

CHAPTER TEN

ALL that week Sophie tried to talk to Guy about Harriet Ridgeway, but each time her nerve failed. They were busy working on a libel suit which had sprung out of a series of articles written by Tom Birny on the current East End gangs. Tom had dug up some statistics on a series of cases in the courts involving members of these gangs: drug-related crimes, vice-related crimes, murders. He had managed to link the known criminals to the families they came from and had built up a sort of family tree of crime.

It had been a sensation, especially appearing in an old-established family newspaper like the *Sentinel*, which had hitherto rarely covered crime except with kid gloves.

Members of the families who had no criminal record but were named in the article were threatening to sue the paper now, and Guy had to decide whether or not to pay out-of-court settlements or to defend the case.

Right up to Christmas Eve Sophie was kept very busy processing the background material Tom had given them.

'I'll take a copy home with me and study it in more detail over Christmas,' Guy said as she finally handed the printed pages to him.

'Where will you spend your Christmas?'

'With my family, in Leicestershire,' he absently told her, flicking through the document he held.

She watched him, wishing she knew what went on inside his head. Harriet said Guy didn't love her and never had—but was that true? Perhaps Harriet believed it, but Sophie couldn't help being doubtful. Why would Guy pretend to be engaged to her unless he cared about her? A masquerade of that sort might so easily have backfired, for both of them—Guy must have agreed to it for very pressing reasons and the only one that made any real sense was that he had been secretly in love with Harriet, even though he knew that she didn't feel the same about him.

But what about Valerie? Sophie's amber eyes darkened as she thought back to the night of the engagement party, and Guy telling her that he was in love with Valerie Knight. He couldn't be in love with both of them! Or could he?

He laughed suddenly and said without looking up, 'This stuff is unbelievable! Where on earth did Birny get it all?'

'Police records, mainly,' she said, watching his profile. He puzzled her deeply. His features were almost austere, his manner cool and controlled—but Guy's feelings were a complicated jigsaw puzzle and Sophie had never been good at jigsaws.

'There's far more to it than that!' said Guy. 'He's careful not to tag any of his direct quotes, or hint at the identity of his informants, but it's obvious that somebody really opened up to him.'

'He seems to know a lot of criminals, he grew up in the East End, and, of course, his job has meant that he's met a lot more.' Sophie thought of Andreas Kirk. His job meant that he had got to know hundreds of criminals, too—and he stayed on casually friendly terms with them, from what she had seen. Small wonder Harriet Ridgeway was afraid her father wouldn't accept him as a son-in-law!

He wanted Guy. Guy was ultra-respectable, came from a wealthy landed family, Harriet said, and her father loved the thought of her joining them. Sophie sighed, thinking of her own eccentric, bohemian family. She loved them all dearly, but they wouldn't fit in with the sort of family Guy apparently came from.

Valerie wouldn't have fitted in, either. Had Guy ever really been in love with Valerie? And what about herself?

Dark colour filled her face. She hated to remember what had happened the night Gib and Valerie got engaged, especially her own part in those events; but she had to try to work this out. She wanted to understand Guy and his motives for what he did.

Part of her mind mocked her cynically. Was she kidding? It wasn't hard to work his motives out—in fact, they were crystal-clear! She had been upset and Guy had taken advantage of that, to try to get her into bed. Opportunistic bastard!

He obviously didn't even feel guilty; probably told himself that most men would do the same, that he had been trying to be kind, trying to comfort her. A real Father Christmas. And, after all, she hadn't fought him, had she? No. She had been a very yielding victim.

Sophie hated to remember it, but she was too honest to deny it. She had wanted Guy that night and, looking back with searing clarity, she saw that she had always found him very attractive, she had always wanted him, even when she had believed herself to be in love with Gilbey Collingwood.

Why did she keep falling for the wrong man, though? She grimaced, turning to look out of the office window. She didn't understand herself—how could she ever hope to understand Guy?

With dismay she saw that it was snowing again, great white flakes blowing and whirling across the open walkways and the plaza. Even the Thames had an icy sheen although it hadn't actually frozen over here, in London, as it had in narrower reaches of the river.

Guy came up behind her to stare out, too. 'Damn it, not more snow!' His voice was deep with irritation. 'The roads are going to be icy, and I've got a long drive ahead of me if I'm going to get to my parents' home tonight.'

'Maybe you should leave early?'

He sighed. 'I can't. I promised to talk to Nick Caspian before he left. His plane leaves at four o'clock, but he's out to lunch at the moment, and I can't see him until he gets back.'

'Where's he going for Christmas?'

'San Francisco.' Guy laughed shortly. 'If the airports haven't all shut down because of the snow!' He looked at the snow again, groaning. 'I should have left yesterday but I thought the weather was going to improve. If this goes on much longer, I shall be spending Christmas in my flat alone.' He shot her a sideways look, eyes mocking. 'Unless you invite me to join your family!'

Her pulses beat a fast tattoo. 'It wouldn't be a restful Christmas; my family are an oddball collection.'

'Like you, you mean?' he teased and she pretended to laugh.

'Afraid so!'

She longed to have him with her at Christmas; the idea made her weak with joy, yet at the same time she knew just what her family would make of his presence. She had never brought a man home for Christmas before. They would be arranging her wedding before she had finished introducing Guy.

She gave him a secret, uncertain look. 'Talking about families . . . I met Harriet Ridgeway the other day.'

She picked up Guy's surprise, felt him stiffen; he turned to look at her fixedly. 'Harriet? Did you? Where?'

'In a pub. She was having a drink with Gib.'

Guy's face tightened, his cold eyes hard. 'And you just happened to be there, too? Are you still seeing him? I thought you were trying to forget him, dating every man who asked you! Didn't it work? For God's sake, Sophie, where's your pride? He belongs to someone else now.'

'I was not seeing Gib!' she threw back, very flushed. Why should she feel guilty? She hadn't been playing complicated games of love—he had! 'I was doing Christmas shopping and I went into this pub and there they were,' she said. 'Gib introduced me, and when

Harriet heard I was your secretary she asked me to talk to you...'

As her voice faded away Guy's eyes narrowed on her face. 'Asked you to talk to me about what?'

Sophie couldn't meet his eyes now, she looked down, her fingers nervously fidgeting with a strand of wilful hair.

'She...she wants to get married and...there's you...' She took a deep breath. 'She told me that her father thinks she's going to marry you, but...but she said it was just a sham engagement...'

'It was,' Guy drily said, his cool eyes fixed on her profile. 'We dated for some months, and her father obviously thought we were heading for marriage and kept talking as if it was a settled thing. Harriet seemed to be serious, too, and somehow or other I found myself getting engaged to her, but I never got round to buying her a ring, and we didn't set a date; neither of us wanted to marry yet. We told her father we would wait until we were settled in our careers, and he accepted that as sensible, he's that sort of man. But of course once we were both busy at work, and weren't seeing so much of each other, we gradually drifted apart. I haven't seen her for months and the engagement would have been broken off except that Harriet was nervous of telling her father.'

'She still is nervous of telling him,' said Sophie. 'She doesn't know how to break it to him that she wants to marry someone else.'

'Does she? Who?' Guy sounded startled. Had the revelation hurt him? Sophie couldn't look in his direction; if Guy really cared about Harriet Ridgeway it would be more than she could bear. 'My God, don't tell me Harriet's fallen for Gilbey Collingwood, too? I know she has a flat right next door to him and sees quite a bit of him——'

'No, of course not!' Sophie said impatiently. 'She wants to marry Andreas Kirk.'

For a moment there was a silence like a thunderstorm; heavy and pregnant with violence, then Guy's voice exploded, making her nerves leap.

'Is this a joke?'

'D-don't shout at me!' she stammered, trying not to tremble visibly. When he was in that mood he terrified her. 'And no, it isn't a joke. It's very serious!'

Guy's mouth twisted cynically. 'Oh, yes? If it's so serious, why was he dating you?'

That was a question she would have preferred him not to ask. The answer was too embarrassing. Very flushed, she muttered,

'He was curious about you.'

Guy gave a great crack of laughter. 'You're kidding!'

She glared at him, face burning, lips tight.

His eyes mocked. 'How very galling for you.'

'I knew he was up to something all the time,' Sophie defended.

'Of course you did,' Guy said, grinning.

'He didn't pull the wool over my eyes. I realised there was something odd about the way he kept questioning me about you! I guessed he was up to something, but I couldn't guess what! How could I when I didn't even know Harriet Ridgeway existed or had anything to do with you?'

'How on earth did she meet him?' Guy thought aloud, frowning. 'He's not her type.' He laughed angrily. 'And he certainly isn't Judge Ridgeway's. The old man will go spare. Harriet must have lost her mind.'

'She's certainly lost her heart, anyway,' Sophie said. 'I'm all for Harriet, frankly. Why should she marry a man simply because her father approves of him? Or vice versa. Her father's behaving like a stuffed owl, a throwback to the Victorians.'

'That's more or less what he is,' Guy agreed. 'But she is going to have to tell her father sooner or later, if she means to marry Kirk, and then he's going to be so furious he's likely to have a stroke or a heart attack.'

Sophie took a deep breath. 'She realises that. That's why she wants you to tell him.'

'Me?' Guy's voice cracked like a whip, making her jump.

Hurriedly she stammered 'W-well, it m-makes sense, you know. She says he thinks the world of you and you could persuade him to accept anything, even another man for a son-in-law. If you tell the judge that you no longer want to marry Harriet yourself, that the engagement is off for good, you're just good friends now—then she thinks he would be more likely to accept Andreas.'

'He wouldn't let her marry Kirk if he was the last man on earth! The old boy hates him. When he's sitting on one of Kirk's cases it always makes the papers because the two of them fight like tigers all the time. It makes great copy, but it isn't just play-acting. Ridgeway really cannot stand the sight of Kirk.'

Sophie bit her lip. 'Oh.'

Guy suddenly laughed. 'But I'll have a chat with the old boy, after Christmas. I can't wait to see his face when he hears he's going to have Kirk, of all men, for his son-in-law. He may eat his wig.'

She chuckled. 'Oh, you'll talk him round; you're good at talking people into doing what you want them to do.'

'Am I?' The soft voice made her tense up, warily conscious of him. 'I haven't had much luck talking you into doing what I want, have I?' Guy murmured and Sophie swallowed.

Looking at her watch, she said hurriedly, 'Well, I've finished all my work now; can I go? I have a couple of last-minute Christmas presents to buy, then I have to get home to finish the preparations—the family will be descending on us tonight and the house isn't really ready yet. Uncle Theo does his best, but he's so absent-minded. He starts to put up decorations and halfway through remembers a detail he just has to put into his book and goes off to scribble a note down, then forgets to come back.'

'Why are you gabbling, Sophie?' Guy asked in that soft, dangerous voice. 'Is something bothering you?'

'If you had a dozen relatives arriving for Christmas in a few hours, you would be hot and bothered, too,' she said breathlessly.

There was a brief silence, then, 'OK, then, off you go,' Guy said in a curt tone. 'And have a good Christmas.'

Sophie put on her coat and wrapped a red woollen scarf around her head, the long knitted ends flung back over her shoulders; collected her handbag and a shopping bag full of Christmas gifts.

'Have a wonderful Christmas yourself,' she said, lingering. 'Drive carefully on the motorway.'

Guy took a step towards her, then the phone rang and he laughed shortly, leaning over to pick it up.

Sophie took a silver-foil wrapped present from her shopping bag and dropped it on Guy's desk, then fled before he had time to pick it up.

Just after seven o'clock that evening she was busy making a final batch of mince pies in the kitchen when Uncle Theo came out from under the cupboard under the stairs which housed his wine, singing happily, several bottles of Hungarian wine under each arm. It was unfortunate that just at that second his cat, Violet, provoked his dog, Stanislaus, into chasing her across the room.

Uncle Theo didn't have enough warning to stop. In mid-step he tripped over Stanislaus and went flying. Luckily, he fell on to Sophie, who was flung forward on top of her tray of mince pies, crushing them hopelessly. At least Uncle Theo wasn't hurt, however, and only Sophie's dignity was dented when he struggled to his feet, she sat up, and he began to laugh in hiccuping gusts at her face and hair covered in mincemeat and squashed pastry.

'You look...oh, sorry, but you do look...so funny...'
he whooped, and then stopped as they both realised
something.

The real casualty was the wine. Only one bottle wasn't
smashed. The kitchen was a battlefield of broken glass
and red wine.

Stanislaus yelped and, tail down, crawled under a
chair. The cat climbed, spitting and yowling, on top of
a tall kitchen cabinet and crouched there, balefully
staring down at the mess.

Sophie and Uncle Theo stared too, making horrified,
moaning noises. 'Oh, no...no, no...'

Naturally, that was the moment when their guests
chose to arrive. The doorbell chimed loudly and they
looked at each other, still groaning.

'They would come now!' said Uncle Theo. 'Look at
this place...why does this have to happen to me?'

The doorbell rang louder.

'I'm coming, I'm coming,' shouted Uncle Theo,
stamping off.

Sophie was picking bits of mince pie out of her hair
and off her eyelashes. She went over to get some kitchen
roll to wipe her face with and then heard Guy's voice
behind her and spun round, in utter consternation.

He came into the kitchen and stopped dead, his jaw
dropping.

'What are you doing here?' wailed Sophie as he looked
around the room at the wine lake and shattered bottles.

'What have *you* been doing is the real question!'

Uncle Theo was mournful. 'It was an accident, I fell
over the dog and...well, never mind. Where am I going
to get some more wine, at this hour, on Christmas Eve?
My wine merchant shut at five; gone home to his family.
Five bottles of a good wine, that's what you see on that
floor. Isn't that a tragic sight?'

'Very,' said Guy, looking under the chair where
Stanislaus lay. 'By the way, did you know your dog
drank?'

Uncle Theo bent and peered; Stanislaus was quietly lapping up some wine that had flowed under his chair.

'Stop that, you canine horror!' shouted Uncle Theo, grabbing a broom and pushing it under the chair to drive the dog out of cover. 'Get into the sitting-room, you!' he said, sweeping the dog across the room and closing the door on him.

Sophie turned her back on Guy, hurriedly scrubbing away at her face with damp kitchen roll. Why did he have to walk in here when she looked like that?

'Don't do your face on my account,' he teased, laughing. 'I like you that way. Very festive.'

Sophie said with remote dignity, 'You still haven't told me why you're here.'

'He's come to wish us a Happy Christmas!' Uncle Theo said warmly, giving her a reproving look. 'Don't be a Scrooge, Sophie!'

Guy smiled at him. 'I was going home for Christmas, myself, sir, but I decided not to risk driving in this blizzard; the police are giving out warnings about unnecessary journeys and long traffic jams and multiple accidents on the motorways, so I decided to have Christmas on my own this year. I can talk to my family on the phone on Christmas Day.'

Uncle Theo's eyes moistened with instant sadness. 'Christmas alone? No, no, we couldn't let you be alone at Christmas, could we, Sophie?'

Guy met her rebellious eyes and read in them her retort. Couldn't we? she silently told him. Why not?

'Oh, I'll be fine,' he said bravely, though smiling his gratitude at Uncle Theo. 'I have a frozen chicken in the freezer. I didn't buy any vegetables or salad, as I was planning to be away for some days, but I have plenty of frozen junk food. I'll manage. I'll get a lot of work done, anyway.'

Uncle Theo stared accusingly at Sophie, who pretended to be stricken with blindness.

Guy looked down at what he was carrying—a square, gift-wrapped parcel with a big floppy green silk ribbon bow on top.

'Oh, yes, this is for you, Sophie,' he said, holding it out. 'I'd better be on my way now. Before the roads freeze over for the night.'

Uncle Theo flung a compelling arm around his shoulders. 'You aren't going anywhere, my boy. You are staying here. We have plenty of room, there are spare mattresses piled up ready for tonight, and enough food to feed a multitude.' He turned a reproachful stare on Sophie. 'Tell him to stay, Sophie!'

Reluctantly, she said, 'Yes, please stay, Guy,' in a flat voice.

Guy smiled broadly. 'Well, if you're sure you want me, Sophie...'

Her eyes spat angrily at him, but Uncle Theo was blissfully unaware of any undercurrents.

He was ferreting around under the sink for a bucket and mop. 'We must get this cleaned up before the others arrive! Oh, and I must get hold of some more wine from somewhere. There won't be enough otherwise. Now, I wonder who I could ring? Wait a minute, wait a minute...Ferenc! He's coming tomorrow for lunch; I'll ring him and ask him what he has got in his cellar. Ferenc keeps an excellent cellar.' He beamed triumphantly at Guy. 'Excuse me...please! I must make a phone call.'

He rushed out of the room and Guy took off his snow-dusted coat and then his jacket, undid his tie, loosened his collar, rolled up his shirt-sleeves, and began working on the floor with an efficiency that surprised Sophie.

She washed her face at the sink, dried it then checked on her reflection and picked out the last pieces of mince pie from her hair.

'You came here deliberately, didn't you?' she quietly accused.

Guy was kneeling down, carefully picking up shards of spiky glass and dropping them into the bucket.

'I had to bring you that present.'

'It could have waited.'

'What do you want me to say?' he asked. 'That I needed to see you? OK, I needed to see you. I would have risked that drive if I hadn't been going crazy at the thought of not seeing you for nearly a week.'

She froze, staring down at the table she was washing. Her ears beat with shock.

Guy didn't stop to see what effect his words had had; he was busy checking the whole floor for more broken glass.

He had said it, thought Sophie. He had really said it. But did he mean it?

He disposed of the broken glass, and began mopping up the red wine, wringing out the mop, filling the bucket with clean water.

'I'll wash the floor,' Sophie said, reaching for the mop.

'I love you,' Guy said hoarsely.

'Don't say that if you don't mean it!' Sophie said, shaking.

'I love you,' he said again, not touching her, just looking at her in a way that made her dizzy.

The mop fell to the floor and Guy's arms went round her, holding her close. His head came down and his mouth hunted for hers, found it, kissed her hungrily. Sophie's eyes shut and she briefly yielded, kissing him back, a wild, intense need clamouring inside her.

But she didn't trust him. How could she? She broke away, twisting and turning to escape.

'Do you even know what love is?' she angrily asked him. 'First I thought it was Valerie you were in love with; you said it was! But you tried to get me into bed with you, all the same! And then I found out about Harriet! I don't think you know the first thing about falling in love.'

Guy still held her, their bodies touching, his hands flat against her back. Looking down into her amber eyes, he said huskily, 'You're the first woman I've ever really loved, Sophie...'

She groaned fiercely. 'Don't lie to me!'

'I'm not, it's the truth,' he said. 'With Harriet it was always just fun—we were students, having a good time in between exams; it didn't mean a thing to either of us. Ask her if you don't believe me. The only complication with Harriet was her father's crazy ambitions for her. He wants her to marry money, and he knew my family had that. But I never ever seriously thought of marrying Harriet, any more than she really wanted to marry me.'

She had to accept that, remembering what Harriet had told her. But she asked stiffly, 'And Valerie?'

'Valerie!' he said, making a face. 'Darling, Valerie is fun, she's great for a date, very sexy, every man who sees you with her envies you like hell and that feels good—but I wasn't in love with her, either. I fancied her, yes. OK, I would have gone to bed with her if she hadn't been a damn sight more prim and proper than you might realise. Valerie has a very unjustified reputation as a honey-pot. At a guess I'd say Gilbey Collingwood will be her first.'

Sophie stared incredulously. 'You can't expect me to believe that! She's always got men around her.'

'They cluster, but it doesn't mean they ever get to the honey,' Guy said drily.

'But you told me...that night...after the engagement party, you told me you were in love with her!'

'I told you that because it made it easier for you,' he said.

'Easier for me?' she furiously threw back. 'You mean, easier for you—to get me into bed!'

'I wanted you, yes,' he admitted, his eyes blazing at her, direct and unashamed. 'But I was trying to make you realise something, that night—you were never really in love with Gib Collingwood, he was just a mirage on your horizon. You had confused the two things—finding someone attractive and being in love with them. That was why I made love to you—I was trying to show you that you found me just as attractive as him, you just hadn't realised it. I had to make you admit it.'

A hot flush filled her face. 'I admit nothing!'

A husky, violent sound like the growl of a stalking panther sounded in his throat and he tightened his hold on her, crushing her closer and closer until she could scarcely breathe, his face taut with an emotion intense enough to turn cruel.

'You wanted me that night!'

'No, I——'

One hand shot up and pulled her golden-brown hair backwards, arching her body and tilting her face.

'You wanted me then, you want me now,' Guy ground out between his teeth, staring into her confused, shifting eyes.

'Want...want...' she stammered, tears close now, her lower lip trembling. 'That's all you know about love... wanting——'

His mouth swooped down with a demanding, angry passion that left her helpless, her lips parting, her body slackening into a shuddering surrender. She felt his hands run down over her slowly from neck to breast, from waist to thigh, a silky, exploring caress that nearly drove her out of her mind. Sophie couldn't fight any more; she gave in with a moan, her arms going round his neck, kissing him back passionately.

'Sophie...' he groaned against her lips. 'I love you...you've got to believe that. I love you to distraction, it's got worse and worse each day until now I can't bear you out of my sight.'

Tears were creeping down her face, from under her closed lids. Guy felt them and lifted his head, his face aghast. 'Darling...don't. Don't cry, Sophie. I can't stand to see you unhappy...'

'I'm not,' she sobbed. 'I'm happy, you fool.' Her wet lashes lifted and she shakily smiled at him, eyes wide. 'I love you, Guy.'

He caught his breath. 'Oh, God...'

Their mouths met again and as they did they heard a crash as Uncle Theo came hurrying back into the room.

Guy and Sophie sprang apart, flushed and disorientated, but Uncle Theo wasn't looking at them. He was looking round the room in agitation then gave a little sigh of relief, seeing that it was almost back to normal now.

'Wonderful! You've cleared up. Oh, this floor is still wet...where's that mop? I saw the car draw up. Your mother and father are here, Sophie. I'll finish this floor—go and let them in and help them with the luggage...'

'I'll carry that in,' Guy said, following her to the door. Out of sight of Uncle Theo he caught her hand and squeezed it. 'Will we ever get a second alone all over Christmas, with your whole family around us? Tell me again that you love me, quick, before we open the door.'

'I love you,' she whispered.

'I love you,' Guy said, and they kissed in the dark of the hallway, while her family began ringing the doorbell, and in the kitchen Uncle Theo sang loud carols of Christmas joy.

HARLEQUIN **PRESENTS**®

BARBARY WHARF

Charlotte Lamb is one of Harlequin's best-loved and bestselling authors. Her extraordinary career, in which she has written more than one hundred books, has helped shape the face of romance fiction around the world.

Born in the East End of London, Charlotte spent her early childhood moving from relative to relative to escape the bombings of World War II. After working as a secretary in the BBC's European department, she married a political reporter who wrote for the *Times*. Charlotte recalls that it was at his suggestion that she began to write "because it was one job I could do without having to leave our five children." Charlotte and her family now live in a beautiful home on the Isle of Man. It is the perfect setting for an author who creates characters and stories that delight romance readers everywhere.

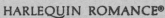

HARLEQUIN ✦ PRESENTS®

A Year
DOWN UNDER

In 1993, Harlequin Presents celebrates the land down under. In March, let us take you to Northland, New Zealand, in THE GOLDEN MASK by Robyn Donald, Harlequin Presents #1537.

Eden has convinced herself that Blade Hammond won't give her a second look. The grueling demands of trying to keep the sheep station running have left her neither the money nor the time to spend on pampering herself. Besides, Blade still considers her a child who needs protecting. Can Eden show him that she's really a woman who needs his love...?

Share the adventure—and the romance— of A Year Down Under!

Available this month in
A YEAR DOWN UNDER

NO GENTLE SEDUCTION
by Helen Bianchin
Harlequin Presents #1527
Wherever Harlequin books are sold.

YDUF

ROMANCE IS A YEARLONG EVENT!

Celebrate the most romantic day of the year with MY VALENTINE! (February)

CRYSTAL CREEK
When you come for a visit Texas-style, you won't want to leave! (March)

Celebrate the joy, excitement and adjustment that comes with being JUST MARRIED! (April)

Go back in time and discover the West as it was meant to be . . . UNTAMED—Maverick Hearts! (July)

LINGERING SHADOWS
New York Times bestselling author Penny Jordan brings you her latest blockbuster. Don't miss it! (August)

BACK BY POPULAR DEMAND!!!
Calloway Corners, involving stories of four sisters coping with family, business and romance! (September)

FRIENDS, FAMILIES, LOVERS
Join us for these heartwarming love stories that evoke memories of family and friends. (October)

Capture the magic and romance of Christmas past with HARLEQUIN HISTORICAL CHRISTMAS STORIES! (November)

WATCH FOR FURTHER DETAILS IN ALL HARLEQUIN BOOKS!

"BARBARY WHARF" SWEEPSTAKES
OFFICIAL RULES — NO PURCHASE NECESSARY

1. To enter each drawing complete the appropriate Offical Entry Form. Alternatively, you may enter any drawing by hand printing on a 3″ × 5″ card (mechanical reproductions are not acceptable) your name, address, daytime telephone number and prize for which that entry is being submitted (Wedgwood Tea Set, $1,000 Shopping Spree, Sterling Silver Candelabras, Royal Doulton China, Crabtree & Evelyn Gift Baskets or Sterling Silver Tray) and mailing it to: Barbary Wharf Sweepstakes, P.O. Box 1397, Buffalo, NY 14269-1397.

No responsibility is assumed for lost, late or misdirected mail. For eligibility all entries must be sent separately with first class postage affixed and received by 11/23/92 for Wedgwood Tea Set (approx. value $543) or, at winner's option, $500 cash drawing; 12/22/92 for the $1,000 Shopping Spree at any retail establishment winner selects or, at winner's option, $1,000 cash drawing; 1/22/93 for Sterling Silver Candelabras (approx. value $875) or, at winner's option, $700 cash drawing, 2/22/93 for the Royal Doulton China service for 8 (approx. value $1,060) or, at winner's option, $900 cash drawing; 3/22/93 for the 12 monthly Crabtree & Evelyn Gift Baskets (approx. value $960) or, at winner's option, $750 cash drawing and, 4/22/93 for the Sterling Silver Tray (approx. value $1,200) or, at winner's option, $750 cash drawing. All winners will be selected in random drawings to be held within 7 days of each drawing eligibility deadline.

A random drawing from amongst all eligible entries received for participation in any or all drawings will be held no later than April 29, 1993 to award the Grand Prize of a 10 day trip for two (2) to London, England (approx. value $6,000) or, at winner's option, $6,000 cash. Travel option includes 10 nights accommodation at the Kensington Park Hotel, Continental breakfast daily, theater tickets for 2, plus round trip airfare and $1,000 spending money; air transportation is from commercial airport nearest winner's home; travel must be completed within 12 months of winner notification, and is subject to space and accommodation availability; travellers must sign and return a Release of Liability prior to traveling.

2. Sweepstakes offer is open only to residents of the U.S. (except Puerto Rico), and Canada who are 21 years of age or older, except employees and immediate family members of Torstar Corp., its affiliates, subsidiaries, and all agencies, entities and persons connected with the use, marketing, or conduct of this sweepstakes. All federal, state, provincial, municipal and local laws apply. Offer void wherever prohibited by law. Taxes and/or duties are the sole responsibility of the winner. Any litigation within the province of Quebec respecting the conduct and awarding of a prize may be submitted to the Régie des loteries et courses du Quebec. All prizes will be awarded; winners will be notified by mail. No substitution of prizes is permitted. Winner selection is under the supervision of D.L. Blair, Inc., an independent judging organization whose decisions are final. Chances of winning in any drawing are dependent upon the number of eligible entries received. All prizes are valued in U.S. currency.

3. Potential winners must sign and return an Affidavit of Eligibility within 30 days of notification. In the event of non-compliance within this time period, the prize may be awarded to an alternate winner. Any prize or prize notification returned as undeliverable may result in the awarding of that prize to an alternate winner. By acceptance of their prize, winners consent to the use of their names, photographs or their likenesses for purposes of advertising, trade and promotion on behalf of Torstar Corp. without further compensation to the winner unless prohibited by law. Canadian winners must correctly answer a time-limited arithmetical question in order to be awarded a prize.

4. For a list of winners (available after 5/31/93), send a separate stamped, self-addressed envelope to: Barbary Wharf Sweepstakes Winners, P.O. Box 4526, Blair, NE 68009.

This month's special prize:

**A Gift Basket of English Delicacies—
Every Month for a Year!**

If you're the winner, every month for 12 months you'll receive a fabulous gift with English delicacies from Crabtree & Evelyn. The baskets will include such luxurious treats as English chocolates, cookies, preserves, honey, exotic teas and more.

The Grand Prize:

An English Holiday for Two!

Visit London and tour the neighborhoods where the characters in *Barbary Wharf* work and fall in love. Visit the fabulous shops, the museums, the Tower of London and Buckingham Palace...enjoy theater and fine dining. And as part of your ten-day holiday, you'll be invited to lunch with the author, Charlotte Lamb! Round-trip air-fare for two, first-class hotels, and meals are all included.

BARBARY WHARF

SWEEPSTAKES

OFFICIAL

ENTRY FORM

THIS MONTH'S SPECIAL PRIZE:

A Gift Basket of Jams, Chocolates & More—
Every Month for a Year

NOTICE》 Entry must be received by March 22, 1993.
Winner will be notified by March 30, 1993.

GRAND PRIZE:

A Vacation to England!

See prize descriptions on the back of this entry form.

Fill in your name and address below and return this
entry form with your invoice in the reply envelope provided.
Good luck!

NAME

ADDRESS

CITY   STATE/PROV.   ZIP/POSTAL CODE

( )

DAYTIME PHONE NUMBER   (AREA CODE)

BW-M5